THE HERITAGE CLUB

Sandglass

NUMBER II-R: 41

ISSUED MONTHLY TO THE MEMBERS OF
THE HERITAGE CLUB
NORWALK, CONNECTICUT

At Voltaire's Supper Table

CARON DE BEAUMARCHAIS, author of *Le Barbier de Seville, Le Mariage de Figaro,* and other works, tried his hand at many occupations, including that of publisher. In order to publish Voltaire, whose work was outlawed by the French authorities, he set up his printing press outside France, at Kehl, just across the Rhine from Strasbourg.

By writing *Candide,* Voltaire enriched himself; Beaumarchais ruined himself in publishing it.

I

VOLTAIRE was sixty-five when he wrote the book. Now—to quote from Paul Morand's Gallic introduction—it is said that in France men are young only on the threshold of old age. Then only are they rid of life's encumbrances, the pressure of the family and education, the worries of a career obstructed by their seniors, the dark importunities of the *libido,* and can at last acquire the limpid gaze and carefree laugh, the free-and-easiness of poise and right of thinking out loud, the moral versatility and cast-iron digestion for the assimilation of ideas—in a word, the intellectual faculties in their finest fettle—which elsewhere are attributes of youth but are, in France, considered the privilege of age.

Voltaire began to write "youthfully" when he was past sixty. One British traveller declared that to see Voltaire at his best one had to be asked to sup with him; "at supper he unbent." It was in the evening of his life, likewise, that Voltaire was at his most communicative; thus to read *Candide* is to be a guest at Voltaire's supper-table.

He was born in 1694, when France held the first place in Europe and the French monarchy was absolute: he died in 1778, within a few years of the Revolution that swept the monarchy out of existence and brought the armies of Europe to Paris. During the intervening years he suffered nearly every change of fortune: he was imprisoned, he was a favorite at Versailles, he was beaten by footmen, he was an honored guest at Potsdam, he was ranked above Corneille and Racine, he saw his books burnt by the hangman, he was elected a member of the Academy.

[1]

He lived in a sort of exile, he died after a sort of apotheosis in Paris. Yet these vicissitudes were natural incidents in the long war he waged against the worn-out forms of thought which he did more than any other man to destroy.

The name that has become famous was not his own: it is an anagram constructed of *Arouet l.j. (le jeune)*, adopted early in his career in place of the one under which, as he said, he had been too unhappy. He was born François-Marie Arouet, the son of a notary in Paris, and educated at the Jesuit College of Louis-le-Grand. His precocious genius, his zest for life, won him a place in the frivolous society of the Regency, where he developed the poetic talent that is the special mark of his earlier years. Imprisonment in 1717 for a satire he had not written was the prelude to an experience that had more lasting consequences. Permitted to expiate his crime by exile, he went to England in 1726.

"During the two generations," so says Buckle in *The History of Civilization,* "which elapsed between the death of Louis XIV and the outbreak of the Revolution, there was hardly a Frenchman of eminence who did not either visit England or learn English, while many did both."

Voltaire did both. He went to the England of Pope and Swift, of Bolingbroke and Chesterfield: in comparison with the France of that time, a home of political liberty and freedom of speech, of scientific discovery and philosophic thought. Voltaire made the acquaintance of all the men of note. He read Shakespeare and Milton; he studied Newton and Locke. In 1729 he was permitted to return home. To quote Lord Morley: "He left France a poet, he returned to it a sage."

An almost unparalleled literary activity occupied the whole of his long life. His works fill ninety volumes. For more than sixty years plays, poems, history, philosophy, political studies, physics, metaphysics, novels, literary criticism, rolled from his pen, and in addition he occupied his leisure with a vast correspondence filling over seventeen fat volumes!

The great lesson he sought to teach was that of tolerance, always of tolerance.

With the idea of making France and the world more fit for men to inhabit, he set to driving his sharp pen into the vitals of every intolerance, of every bigot, of every tyranny he could find.

Voltaire's life was therefore one long fight. He considered his pen far more a useful tool with which to carve channels through which his creed of tolerance might flow, a weapon with which to kill the devils of bigotry and injustice, than as an instrument for making things to delight the world and enhance his own renown. To him Fame was always less important than Right. And so *Candide* is a window through which those who had eyes to see might observe contemporary ignorance and infamy.

This is true of all of Voltaire's novels. Whenever he seems to be laughing most, then he is most serious, in the most deadly earnest. Voltaire's laughter was barbed; it never shot out from his mind without striking to kill. In his time (as perhaps in all times!) it was dangerous to tell the truth, for men live by lies. But what a happy thought it was to force men to read the truth for their own amusement, without a suspicion at first that they were reading their own indictment, carried on from page to page by pure enjoyment of Voltaire's frolicking, until when the last page was read something of the author's profound meaning started to glimmer in the reader's mind, to illumine his soul!

"Few books of philosophy are more useful than the philosophical novel," to quote Condorcet. "They are read by frivolous men, to whom the mere name of philosophy is repugnant."

Well, *Candide* is a philosophic treatise. But (as Paul Morand justly points out) "it is homily that reads like a repartee, a masterpiece essentially French in its knack of putting big problems in small bottles, of popularizing without truckling to the popular, of contriving to wear the livery of tolerance as if it were a silken robe; of being witty at the expense of wit. . . .

"*Candide* is the fine flower of a man who himself was the fine flower of his age; of the writer whose works are a sort of anthology of the fine flowers of his days, culled from English, German, Japanese, Dutch, Italian, and Patagonian gardens, and of the most fertile ideas of his generation. It is delightful testament of a smiling pessimist."

And *Candide* is crammed with adventures, too: the adventures of Candide the blessed, who, advancing from theory to theory, by way of peril and disaster, won through to wisdom and Nirvana. It is even a sequence of burlesque, breath-taking catastrophes developed in a long *crescendo* that gradually dies down and comes to a harmonious close in the rustic setting of a little garden.

II

ALTHOUGH its publication ruined its first publisher, *Candide* is a work which made its author a model for later writers, a work which stirred whole continents, a work which must inevitably find its place in every list of the great classics.

That is why the members of this Club are now receiving their copies of an edition of *Candide* which is illustrated by

Sylvain Sauvage. The edition results from a plan—devised back in the thirties—for producing in a single series of volumes "The Ten Great French Romances." As one of France's leading men-of-letters, André Maurois was approached with the request that he organize a committee of ten French men-of-letters who would select "The Ten Great French Romances" and provide fresh introductions for these ten great books. That committee met in M. Maurois's handsome apartment in the Bois, and made its list—and *Candide* inevitably found its place in the list.

Yet that is only part of the story.

Ten great French artists were then approached, with the request that each of them select one of these "Ten Great French Romances" for illustration. Sylvain Sauvage elected to illustrate *Candide*.

That was in 1939. In 1949, Sylvain Sauvage passed on to his Maker. At his death he was among the most eminent of French artists. And his work is well known in this country, too. As long ago as 1934, he entered a competition in book illustration which The Limited Editions Club conducted; he submitted a series of illustrations for Anatole France's *At the Sign of the Queen Pédauque*. These drawings were done in water colors, they were pretty to look upon, they were full of a literary understanding of the text, they were shot through with a satiric wit. The judges gave them one of the prizes.

Sauvage's illustrations have since embellished such Heritage Press editions as *Romeo and Juliet* and *Penguin Island*. In his native country, he illustrated Longus' *Daphnis and Chloe, The Songs of Bilitis,* and dozens upon dozens of other volumes.

He was born in Franche-Comté, a province which at the turn of the century was savagely struggling for its independence, a curious country of deep valleys and little rivers abounding in fish, its pine forests circling its lakes and vineyards and pastures and waterfalls-for-industry. Here too were born Victor Hugo, Louis Pasteur, and Rouget de Lisle.

Sauvage's father was an architect, and he studied architecture before World War I. He served eighteen months at the front, and after the war he turned to book illustration. He was sixty-one years of age at his death, and didn't look it: a big robust man with flowing red hair and a flowing black tie in the Bohemian fashion. He devoted his life to the cause of the fine book, and served as director of L'Ecole Estienne, a school which he dedicated to be a conservatory of the arts and technique of the book.

Sylvain Sauvage was expert at engraving in wood and copper and in drawing lithographs on the stone. But his watercolors were so charming that they made him highly popular.

For he knew how to make illustrations which are bookish, which belong within the covers of a book and not upon a wall. But he was also a gentleman of scholarly wit, and the making of pictures for *Candide* proved right up his alley. He made twenty water-colors and carefully planned them for reproduction. Each of these pictures is charming and full of wit; each is a picture to awaken thoughtful laughter. You look at the pictures, and you begin to chuckle with Voltaire himself over the vagaries of a misfit civilization.

He drew them in black, with a brush using black water-color. Then, on photographic prints of the full-page illustrations, Sauvage applied the colors, sometimes four colors on a print. All of the printed sheets were then carefully reproduced to hold the effect of the originals.

These illustrations are Pictures with a capital P. They are Pictures which repay study: and you should never be satisfied with any work of art which does *not* repay study, which satisfies you at one glance.

The text we have used is the translation from the French made by Richard Aldington. Paul Morand, who wrote the introduction, was a playwright, a diplomat, and the author of several witty and polemical novels in the wake of Voltaire. He was one of the committee of ten French men-of-letters who selected The Ten Great French Romances.

For that series, the typographic plans were made by Sir Francis Meynell of London. The type he chose is the Monotype face called Cochin, a modern redrawing of a type originally drawn by the great French printer named Nicolas Cochin at just about the time when Voltaire was writing *Candide*. And Sir Francis has used, as decorations for the type, a series of hand-drawn flourishes which are French in their flavor.

The composition of the type was done in London by the Curwen Press, and the printing was performed in the U.S.A. by The Connecticut Printers of Bloomfield, upon a cream-white paper with an eggshell finish, made specially for this book at the Strathmore mill in West Springfield, Mass.

The binding is in classic three-piece style. For the sides we imported paper from Italy—an unusual paper printed with an allover French pattern of fleurs-de-lis in gold on a colored background. The spine cloth was dyed to match the paper of the sides, then stamped in gold leaf. The binding operations were performed by Tapley-Rutter, that best of all possible binderies in Moonachie, N. J.

THE DIRECTORS

[4]

CANDIDE

FRANCOIS MARIE AROUET DE VOLTAIRE

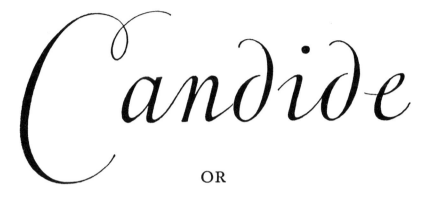

OR

OPTIMISM

Translated from the French by RICHARD ALDINGTON

With an Introduction by PAUL MORAND

and illustrations in colour by

SYLVAIN SAUVAGE

The Heritage Press

NORWALK, CONNECTICUT

PRINTED IN THE UNITED STATES OF AMERICA

THE CONTENTS

PAUL MORAND

A NEW WORLD *needs "young" works. To bring* Candide *to the notice of readers in England and the United States is to introduce them to one of the "youngest" novels of the Old Continent.*

Voltaire was sixty-five when he wrote it.

The truth is that in France men are young only on the threshold of old age. Then only are they rid of life's encumbrances, the pressure of the family and education, the worries of a career obstructed by their seniors, the dark importunities of the libido, *and can at last acquire the limpid gaze and carefree laugh, the free-and-easiness of poise and right of thinking out aloud, the moral versatility and cast-iron digestion for the assimilation of ideas—in a word, the intellectual faculties in their finest fettle—which elsewhere may be attributes of youth but are in France, most certainly, the privilege of age. (Thus in the portraits of Gide as a young man we see a bitter and tormented mouth, bent head, and gaze darkened by introspection; the latest photographs of Gide in the sixties show a man firm-lipped, with forthright eyes and a commanding presence.) Voltaire began to write "youthfully" when he was past sixty. Moore, the British traveller, said of him that to see the patriarch of Ferney at his best one had to be asked to sup with him; "at supper he unbent." And likewise it was in the evening of his life that Voltaire was at his most communicative, and to read* Candide *is to be a guest at Voltaire's supper-table.*

Who does not know the golden tale of Candide's youth? Born in the castle of Baron Thunder-ten-tronckh in Westphalia (the noblest castle in the land, for it possessed a door and even several windows), little Candide was brought up by his tutor, the worthy Doctor Pangloss, on the philosophy of Leibnitz, and inoculated with a firm belief in the pre-ordained harmony of things which, taken with the invincible concatenation of causes and effects, ensures that all that happens cannot but happen for the best, and that therefore "all is for the best in the best of all possible worlds." This famous precept is belied from the first page of Candide *to the last by a positive spate of calamities. To begin with, Candide falls in love with Cunegonde, the Baron's pretty daughter, and snatches a kiss from her; the immediate effect of this cause is a volley of kicks in our hero's posterior which all too literally "boot him out" of the castle, and into life.*

Surprisingly enough (but we are only at the beginning of our geographical surprises), the army of the adjoining country, Bulgaria, is preparing to invade Westphalia. Candide is pressed into the service of the former and drubbed into learning the noble art of warfare. After his first battle he escapes to Holland, where he meets his old tutor Pangloss—a draggled, unrecognizable Pangloss, noseless, earless, with nothing left intact except his optimism. From him Candide hears of the misfortunes of the Thunder-ten-tronckh household, the castle sacked by the Bulgarian soldiery, the Baron, Baroness and their son massacred, Cunegonde raped and disembowelled. "It was all indispensable"—such was the worthy Doctor's summing-up—"for private misfortunes make the public good, so that the more private misfortunes there are, the more everything goes well."

So that everything might go still better, Candide and Pangloss, after being succoured by a charitable anabaptist merchant and entering on a spell of better days, are shipped off to Lisbon by their benefactor and wrecked in sight of port by a "most horrible tempest." Carried ashore on a plank, they all but perish in the Lisbon earthquake and only escape the plague

Candide : The Introduction

that followed it to fall into the hands of the Inquisition, which has Pangloss hanged and Candide given a hundred lashes. Soaked in blood, more dead than alive, he is befriended by an old serving-woman, who binds up his wounds and conducts him to a mysterious, palatial mansion. There, to his wonder and delight, he is welcomed by the beloved Cunegonde who has escaped by a miracle from the Bulgarian soldiery and now, at Lisbon, shares her favours between Issachar the Jew and the Grand Inquisitor. The lovers are caught flagrante delicto by the Jew and the Inquisitor, nuisances whom Candide speedily abates by running his sword through each in turn. Cunegonde cannot believe her eyes. "Heavens, how does it happen that you, who were born so mild, should kill a Jew and a prelate within two minutes?" "My dear young lady," Candide replies, "when a man is in love, jealous, and has been flogged by the Inquisition, he is beside himself!"

The young couple take to flight, accompanied by the old servant who, as it happens, is no less than a daughter of the Pope; kidnapped by pirates in early youth, she went through tribulations beside which Cunegonde's were the merest fleabites. Our heroes embark for the New World, which seems to them the safest place of refuge. Unluckily the Governor of Buenos Ayres, who bears the prodigious name of Don Fernando d'Ibaraa y Figueora y Mascarenes y Lampourdos y Souza, takes the fair Cunegonde into his keeping and falls foul of Candide, who takes refuge in the Jesuit Republic of Paraguay.

As chance fantastically has it, the Jesuit Commandant is none other than Cunegonde's brother who, after escaping the Bulgarian holocaust and passing through a series of adventures, has made good in Paraguay. But he has lost nothing of his Germanic arrogance, for when he learns that Candide, with far less than seventy-two quarterings on his escutcheon, aspires to marry the noble lady Cunegonde, he strikes the presumptuous suitor with his sword. Candide, promptly if unintention-

Candide : The Introduction

ally, runs him through, and takes to the road again. After a terrible journey he reaches the earthly paradise of Eldorado, where peace and wisdom reign, where the dust is gold, the pebbles on the road are diamonds. But Candide prefers Cunegonde to paradise; laden with a vast store of precious stones, he leaves Eldorado and gives half his stock of jewels to his valet Cacambo, telling him to go and rescue Cunegonde and bring her to join him in Venice, "the home of liberty."

On his way there Candide halts at Paris. Voltaire has already made plain to us his opinions of the army, war, courts of justice, Leibnitz's philosophy, the Admiralty, Jesuits, monks, governments, the police, the dishonesty of merchants and the follies of the nobility. Now, Paris gives him an opportunity of dealing faithfully by high society, parasites, literary critics, playwrights and indeed the human race in general.

"Do you think," says Candide to his travelling companion, Martin the philosopher, "that men have always massacred each other as they do to-day? Have they always been liars, cheats, traitors, brigands, weak, flighty, cowardly, envious, gluttonous, drunken, grasping and ambitious; bloody, backbiting, debauched, fanatical, hypocritical and silly?" "Do you not think," Martin replies, "that sparrow-hawks have always eaten the pigeons they came across?"

Venice is the scene of one of the finest and most "modern" episodes of the tale: Candide's supper with six dethroned kings. Cacambo reappears at Venice, but without Cunegonde; after the direst mishaps, she has declined upon the humble task of scullery-maid at Constantinople. Candide hastens there at once. To his wonder, amongst the galley-slaves rowing the ship on which he travels he finds Pangloss, who has escaped the halter, and the Baron, who has recovered from his sword-thrust. (People whom Voltaire "kills" have a way of remaining tolerably fit.) Candide ransoms everybody, including Cunegonde who has grown old and ugly at her menial task,

*and so shrewish that Candide loses his desire to marry her.
But the Baron, keeping the flag of folly flying with a perse-
verance worthy of a better cause, starts in again with objections
to the match. Stung to the quick, Candide has him deported,
marries Cunegonde, buys a farm, and invites his friends to live
with him.*

*Are they happy in the end? No, they are bored; indeed one
day the old woman makes bold to speak as follows:*

*"I'd like to know which is worse, to be raped a hundred
times by negro pirates, to have a buttock cut off, to run the
gauntlet among the Bulgars, to be whipped and hanged in an
auto-da-fé, to be dissected, to row in a galley—in short to
endure all the miseries through which we have passed—or to
remain here doing nothing?"*

" 'Tis a great question," was Candide's reply.

*As for finding an answer to it, they were in despair till
chance brought across their path a worthy mufti who taught
them to cultivate their garden with their own hands and live on
its produce. The morale of the tale is to be found, presumably,
in the conversation between Candide and Pangloss which con-
cludes it.*

*"All events are beautifully linked up in this best of all
possible worlds," said Pangloss. "For if you had not gone
through all these terrible misfortunes, would you now be here,
eating candied citrons and pistachios?"*

*" 'Tis well said," Candide answered, "but we must culti-
vate our gardens."*

*Thus end the adventures of Candide the blessed, who, advan-
cing from theory to theory, by way of peril and disaster, won
through to wisdom and Nirvana.*

We have seen that Candide *is a sequence of burlesque,
breath-taking catastrophes developed in a long* crescendo
*that gradually dies down and comes to a harmonious close in
the rustic setting of a little garden. Critics, according as they*

Candide : The Introduction

judge the work by its tempestuous early phases, or by the dead calm of its final scene, have found in it either an epic of diabolism and cruelty or a pre-Tolstoyan gospel of social salvation. But Voltaire had taken up the cudgels often enough in his time for him to permit himself on this occasion an attitude of ironical neutrality. Born in an epoch that was pitiless par excellence, *the age of Lovelace and Valmont, of the Marquis de Sade and Frederick the Great, of the slave-trade and the Partitions of Poland—born in such an age,* Candide *may well not be a model of loving-kindness, but it was no more cruel than its times. A Frenchman, pen in hand, is rarely kind; at best he teases, and teasing is a mild form of sadism. It has been asserted that Voltaire, out of tenderness of heart, went into a fever on each anniversary of Saint Bartholomew's Eve. That fever would certainly have surprised Candide, philosophical observer of all the ills that man is heir to, who whenever an earthquake, shipwreck or pestilence, a rape or an impalement came to his notice would be more apt to say, like the Surinam negro, "It is the custom." Had he ever been called on to sound a dirge for man's distressful lot, we may be sure he would have rendered it blithely on one of those Peruvian flutes made of a human shin-bone.*

A pupil of the Jesuits, Voltaire was shaped by these past-masters of the lavish and ornate, of the richly moulded period, overlaid with the stuccoed volutes and operatic flourishes of the "macaroni" style. Under their influence alone he would have pressed virtuosity too far and lapsed into the high-falutin—his tragedies are proof of this. But he lived for a while amongst the Puritans; London saved him from going Italianate by opening to him the portals of a wider world. While in his form (which is perfection) Voltaire remained a Latin, he became British in outlook. On landing he went to stay with Lord Bolingbroke at Greenwich and there, appropriately enough, the man who was destined to become the intellectual meridian of an epoch was quick to catch the rhythm of Western Time. It was in England, the first free country, that he learned to think out loud. For though the Englishman dresses for dinner, he puts no starched shirt on his mind. And if eighteenth-century France and indeed Europe were so thoroughly won over to the new outlook on life that had made good in England at the close of the preceding century, the reason is that that outlook was simple and urbane—and every scheme of living that destroys with high good-humour is invincible. That, too, is why on his return from England Voltaire was able to provide France with a new genre: *sermons in smiles and genial revolution.*

*As crammed with adventure as is a plum pudding with currants, sprinkled with the comic names that Ben Jonson had brought into fashion, crowded with Turks and Russians and incredible negroes who seem to have stepped down from a Chippendale screen, as rich in recipes for cosmopolitan life as are Lord Chesterfield's letters, jingling with sequins, sovereigns and maravedis like the purse of a young lord on the Grand Tour, veneered with Lockian metaphysics, polished with Newtonian science and impregnated with that Jew-Dutch atmosphere of Fleet Street, in which the relativity of ideas, the lore of comparative cultures and the dramatic ups-and-downs of the stock-market are plain to read on every face—*Candide *is the* chef-d'oeuvre *of a Londonized Frenchman.*

In the clowning, railing, super-charged, rampageous chronicle that is Candide, *with its ribald horseplay, fisticuffs landing on thickly powdered cheeks, kicks on the seats of silken pantaloons, there is something of the English touch.* Candide *is the* "Volez-vous jouer avec moa" *of Voltaire the pugilist, whose shrewd blows made the greatest European monarchs bite the mat. He is more than the Italian Harlequin; rather the Covent Garden droll, descended in the direct line from the Devil in old English mystery-plays, the classical buffoon with*

Candide : The Introduction

his privilege of knuckle-rapping and imperturbable philosophy —inherited by Pangloss—and his rustic simplicity—illustrated by Cacambo.

The tale of Candide *was born in England, but on one of those days of limpid light when from Dover you can see across to Calais; its local habitation is somewhere in mid-Channel. If* Candide *is a masterpiece marking the climax of a thousand years of intellectual commerce between France and England, this is because it wedded the rugosities of thought then somewhat prevalent in Britain with the formal elegance of French art. How eagerly Voltaire must have read Swift and his "Tale of a Tub," written in 1697, in which the spontaneous flights of fancy and metaphysical humour that made* Candide's *huge success are already plain to see. Never was a great man more shrewdly spoiled than was poor Swift by Voltaire; we have only to read the opening pages of* Candide *to find our appreciation of his vigour, dryness, tartness on the wane; how morbid, pessimistic and crabbed the Dean comes to appear—and how desperately slow! After the description of the Jesuit of Paraguay that of the Presbyterian hardly bears re-reading; when we have come to know the savages called "Oreillons," how find amusement in the company of the Yahoos? One of the amazing things about Voltaire is his rhythm, his* tempo *running true as clockwork. Even Beaumarchais' "repeater," perfected though it is, does not provide such punctual misfortunes, such apt recurrence of calamities, setbacks and mishaps so neatly interlocked.*

"The world," wrote Voltaire, "is a vast shipwreck and man's device, Sauve qui peut!" *Born an Englishman, Candide would surely have killed himself; born French and fathered by a man like Voltaire who made the most of everything, even of that terrestrial happiness in view of which the easy-going eighteenth century broke with Pascal's tragic sense of life, Candide was saved by horticulture, a garden on the*

Candide : The Introduction

shores of the Bosphorus. A life's last chapter justly famed, but proving, as every gardener knows, how little Voltaire knew of nature's ways. No place is more exposed to calamity than is a kitchen garden, and we should need all Candide's breezy optimism to fancy that life's troubles end once one has sown some rows of peas, for we should have to rule out hoar-frosts, shut our eyes to slugs.

Candide *is a philosophic treatise scaled down to the dimensions of an article in the* Dictionnaire Philosophique : *a homily that reads like a repartee, a masterpiece essentially French in its knack of putting big problems in small bottles, popularizing without truckling to the popular, contriving to wear the homespun livery of equity and tolerance as if it were a silken robe; of being witty at the expense of wit, doomed though one may be to display it in every circumstance and field, not excepting that of poetry—a dreadful plight indeed !*

Candide *is the fine flower of a man who himself was the fine flower of his age; of the writer whose works are a sort of anthology of the fine flowers of his days, culled from English, German, Japanese, Dutch, Italian and Patagonian gardens, and of the most fertile ideas of his generation. It is the wholly delightful testament of a smiling pessimist, a healthy hypochondriac, a democrat fawned on by autocrats, a plaintive millionaire, a revolutionary conservative, and an antipoetic poet.*

Candide *is the verdict of a privileged centenarian who has outlived his illusions, the "I-have-had-all-and-all-is-nothing" of a lucky winner of the lottery of letters, the master-stroke of a gambler whose sleight of mind outwitted chance, bested the bank at every spin.*

By writing Candide *Voltaire enriched himself; Beaumarchais ruined himself, publishing* Candide.

CARON DE BEAUMARCHAIS, AUTHOR
OF *LE BARBIER DE SEVILLE, LE
MARIAGE DE FIGARO* AND OTHER
WORKS, TRIED HIS HAND AT MANY
OCCUPATIONS, INCLUDING THAT OF
PUBLISHER. IN ORDER TO PUBLISH
VOLTAIRE, WHOSE WORK WAS OUT-
LAWED BY THE FRENCH AUTHO-
RITIES, HE SET UP HIS PRINTING
PRESS OUTSIDE FRANCE, AT KEHL;
FOR WHICH REASON THIS CELE-
BRATED ISSUE OF *CANDIDE*
BEARS THE INSCRIPTION
EDITION DE KEHL.

◆ TRANSLATOR ◇

Candide, or Optimism

Translated from the German of Dr Ralph
with the additions found in the Doctor's
pocket when he died at Minden
in the year of grace, 1757

CHAPTER I

How Candide was brought up in a noble castle, and how he was expelled from the same

IN the castle of Baron Thunder-ten-tronckh in West-phalia there lived a youth, endowed by Nature with the most gentle character. His face was the expression of his soul. His judgment was quite honest and he was extremely simple-minded; and this was the reason, I think, that he was named Candide. Old servants in the house suspected that he was the son of the Baron's sister and a decent honest gentleman of the neighbourhood, whom this young lady would never marry because he could only prove seventy-one quarterings, and the rest of his genealogical tree was lost, owing to the injuries of time.

The Baron was one of the most powerful lords in Westphalia, for his castle possessed a door and windows. His Great Hall was even decorated with a piece of tapestry. The dogs in his stable-yards formed a pack of hounds when necessary; his grooms were his huntsmen; the village curate was his Grand Almoner. They all called him "My Lord," and laughed heartily at his stories.

The Baroness weighed about three hundred and fifty pounds, was therefore greatly respected, and did the honours of the house with a dignity which rendered her still more respectable. Her daughter Cunegonde, aged seventeen, was rosy-cheeked, fresh, plump and tempting. The Baron's son appeared in every respect worthy of his father. The tutor Pangloss was the oracle of the house,

3

and little Candide followed his lessons with all the candour of his age and character.

Pangloss taught metaphysico-theologo-cosmolonigol-ogy. He proved admirably that there is no effect without a cause and that in this best of all possible worlds, My Lord the Baron's castle was the best of castles and his wife the best of all possible Baronesses.

"'Tis demonstrated," said he, "that things cannot be otherwise; for, since everything is made for an end, everything is necessarily for the best end. Observe that noses were made to wear spectacles; and so we have spectacles. Legs were visibly instituted to be breeched, and we have breeches. Stones were formed to be quarried and to build castles; and My Lord has a very noble castle; the greatest Baron in the province should have the best house; and as pigs were made to be eaten, we eat pork all the year round; consequently, those who have asserted that all is well [1] talk nonsense; they ought to have said that all is for the best."

Candide listened attentively and believed innocently; for he thought Miss Cunegonde extremely beautiful, although he was never bold enough to tell her so. He decided that after the happiness of being born Baron of Thunder-ten-tronckh, the second degree of happiness was to be Miss Cunegonde; the third, to see her every day; and the fourth to listen to Doctor Pangloss, the greatest philosopher of the province and therefore of the whole world.

One day when Cunegonde was walking near the castle, in a little wood which was called The Park, she observed Doctor Pangloss in the bushes, giving a lesson in experimental physics to her mother's waiting-maid, a very pretty and docile brunette. Miss Cunegonde had a great inclination for science and watched breath-

---

[1] Tout est bien, all is well, said Rousseau in his famous attack on Voltaire's poem about the Lisbon earthquake. See Introduction.

lessly the reiterated experiments she witnessed; she observed clearly the Doctor's sufficient reason, the effects and the causes, and returned home very much excited, pensive, filled with the desire of learning,

reflecting that she might be the sufficient reason of young Candide and that he might be hers.

On her way back to the castle she met Candide and blushed; Candide also blushed. She bade him good-morning in a hesitating voice; Candide replied without knowing what he was saying. Next day, when they left the table after dinner, Cunegonde and Candide found themselves behind a screen; Cunegonde dropped her handkerchief, Candide picked it up; she innocently held his hand; the young man innocently kissed the young lady's hand with remarkable vivacity, tenderness and grace; their lips met, their eyes sparkled, their knees trembled, their hands wandered. Baron Thunder-ten-tronckh passed near the screen, and, observing this cause and effect, expelled Candide from the castle by kicking him in the backside frequently and hard. Cunegonde swooned; when she recovered her senses, the Baroness slapped her in the face; and all was in consternation in the noblest and most agreeable of all possible castles.

CHAPTER II

What happened to Candide among the Bulgarians

CANDIDE, expelled from the earthly paradise, wandered for a long time without knowing where he was going, weeping, turning up his eyes to Heaven, gazing back frequently at the noblest of castles which held the most beautiful of young Baronesses; he lay down to sleep supperless between two furrows in the open fields; it snowed heavily in large flakes. The next morning the shivering Candide, penniless, dying of cold and exhaustion, dragged himself towards the neighbouring town, which was called Waldberghoff-trarbk-dikdorff. He halted sadly at the door of an inn. Two men dressed in blue noticed him.

"Comrade," said one, "there's a well-built young man of the right height."

They went up to Candide and very civilly invited him to dinner.

"Gentlemen," said Candide with charming modesty, "you do me a great honour, but I have no money to pay my share."

"Ah, sir," said one of the men in blue, "persons of your figure and merit never pay anything; are you not five feet five tall?"

"Yes, gentlemen," said he, bowing, "that is my height."

"Ah, sir, come to table; we will not only pay your expenses, we will never allow a man like you to be short of money; men were only made to help each other."

"You are in the right," said Candide, "that is what Doctor Pangloss was always telling me, and I see that everything is for the best."

They begged him to accept a few crowns, he took them and wished to give them an IOU; they refused to take it and all sat down to table.

"Do you not love tenderly . . . ."

"Oh, yes," said he. "I love Miss Cunegonde tenderly."

"No," said one of the gentlemen. "We were asking if you do not tenderly love the King of the Bulgarians."

"Not a bit," said he, "for I have never seen him."

"What! He is the most charming of Kings, and you must drink his health."

"Oh, gladly, gentlemen."

And he drank.

"That is sufficient," he was told. "You are now the support, the aid, the defender, the hero of the Bulgarians; your fortune is made and your glory assured."

They immediately put irons on his legs and took him to a regiment. He was made to turn to the right and left, to raise the ramrod and return the ramrod, to take aim, to fire, to double up, and he was given thirty strokes with a stick; the next day he drilled not quite so badly, and received only twenty strokes; the day after, he only had ten and was looked on as a prodigy by his comrades.

Candide was completely mystified and could not make out how he was a hero. One fine spring day he thought he would take a walk, going straight ahead, in the belief that to use his legs as he pleased was a privilege of the human species as well as of animals. He had not gone two leagues when four other heroes, each six feet tall, fell upon him, bound him and dragged him back to a cell. He was asked by his judges whether he would rather be thrashed thirty-six times by the whole regiment or receive a dozen lead bullets at once in his brain. Although he protested that men's wills are free and that he wanted neither one nor the other, he had to make a choice; by virtue of that gift of God which is called *liberty*, he determined to run the gauntlet thirty-six times and actually did so twice. There were two thousand men in the regiment. That made four thousand strokes which laid bare the muscles and nerves from his neck to his backside. As they were about to proceed to a third turn, Candide, utterly exhausted, begged as a favour that they would be so kind as to smash his head; he obtained this favour; they bound his eyes and he was made to kneel down. At that moment the King of the Bulgarians came by and inquired the victim's crime; and as this King was possessed of a vast genius, he perceived from what he learned about Candide that he was a young metaphysician very ignorant in worldly matters, and therefore pardoned him with a clemency which will be praised in all newspapers and all ages. An honest surgeon healed Candide in three weeks with the ointments recommended by Dioscorides.[1] He had already regained a little skin and could walk when the King of the Bulgarians went to war with the King of the Abares.[2]

---

[1] A Greek author of the time of Nero.

[2] The Bulgarians are the Prussians and the Abares the French. The King of vast genius is Frederick the Great, whose recruiting methods are glanced at in this chapter.

CHAPTER III

How Candide escaped from the Bulgarians and what became of him

NOTHING could be smarter, more splendid, more brilliant, better drawn up than the two armies. Trumpets, fifes, hautboys, drums, cannons, formed a harmony such as has never been heard even in hell. The cannons first of all laid flat about six thousand men on each side; then the musketry removed from the best of worlds some nine or ten thousand blackguards who infested its surface. The bayonet also was the sufficient reason for the death of some thousands of men. The whole might amount to thirty thousand souls. Candide, who trembled like a philosopher, hid himself as well as he could during this heroic butchery.

At last, while the two Kings each commanded a Te Deum in his camp, Candide decided to go elsewhere to reason about effects and causes. He clambered over heaps of dead and dying men and reached a neighbouring village, which was in ashes; it was an Abare village which the Bulgarians had burned in accordance with international law. Here, old men dazed with blows watched the dying agonies of their murdered wives who clutched their children to their bleeding breasts; there, disembowelled girls who had been made to satisfy the natural appetites of heroes gasped their last sighs; others, half-burned, begged to be put to death. Brains were scattered on the ground among dismembered arms and legs.

Candide fled to another village as fast as he could; it belonged to the Bulgarians, and Abarian heroes had

10

treated it in the same way. Candide, stumbling over quivering limbs or across ruins, at last escaped from the theatre of war, carrying a little food in his knapsack, and never forgetting Miss Cunegonde. His provisions were all gone when he reached Holland; but, having heard that every one in that country was rich and a Christian, he had no doubt at all but that he would be as well treated as he had been in the Baron's castle before he had been expelled on account of Miss Cunegonde's pretty eyes.

He asked an alms of several grave persons, who all replied that if he continued in that way he would be shut up in a house of correction to teach him how to live.

He then addressed himself to a man who had been discoursing on charity in a large assembly for an hour on end. This orator, glancing at him askance, said:

"What are you doing here? Are you for the good cause?"

"There is no effect without a cause," said Candide modestly. "Everything is necessarily linked up and arranged for the best. It was necessary that I should be expelled from the company of Miss Cunegonde, that I ran the gauntlet, and that I beg my bread until I can earn it; all this could not have happened differently."

"My friend," said the orator, "do you believe that the Pope is Anti-Christ?"

"I had never heard so before," said Candide, "but whether he is or isn't, I am starving."

"You don't deserve to eat," said the other. "Hence, rascal; hence, you wretch; and never come near me again."

The orator's wife thrust her head out of the window and seeing a man who did not believe that the Pope was Anti-Christ, she poured on his head a full. . . . . O Heavens! To what excess religious zeal is carried by ladies!

A man who had not been baptized, an honest Ana-

11

baptist named Jacques, saw the cruel and ignominious treatment of one of his brothers, a featherless two-legged creature with a soul; he took him home, cleaned him up, gave him bread and beer, presented him with two florins, and even offered to teach him to work at the manufacture of Persian stuffs which are made in Holland. Candide threw himself at the man's feet, exclaiming:

"Doctor Pangloss was right in telling me that all is for the best in this world, for I am vastly more touched by your extreme generosity than by the harshness of the gentleman in the black cloak and his good lady."

The next day when he walked out he met a beggar covered with sores, dull-eyed, with the end of his nose fallen away, his mouth awry, his teeth black, who talked huskily, was tormented with a violent cough and spat out a tooth at every cough.

CHAPTER IV

How Candide met his old master in philosophy, Doctor Pangloss, and what happened

CANDIDE, moved even more by compassion than by horror, gave this horrible beggar the two florins he had received from the honest Anabaptist, Jacques. The phantom gazed fixedly at him, shed tears and threw its arms round his neck. Candide recoiled in terror.

"Alas!" said the wretch to the other wretch, "don't you recognise your dear Pangloss?"

"What do I hear? You, my dear master! You, in this horrible state! What misfortune has happened to you? Why are you no longer in the noblest of castles? What has become of Miss Cunegonde, the pearl of young ladies, the masterpiece of Nature?"

"I am exhausted," said Pangloss. Candide immediately took him to the Anabaptist's stable where he gave him a little bread to eat; and when Pangloss had recovered:

"Well!" said he, "Cunegonde?"

"Dead," replied the other.

At this word Candide swooned; his friend restored him to his senses with a little bad vinegar which happened to be in the stable. Candide opened his eyes.

"Cunegonde dead! Ah! best of worlds, where are you? But what illness did she die of? Was it because she saw me kicked out of her father's noble castle?''

"No," said Pangloss. "She was disembowelled by Bulgarian soldiers, after having been raped to the limit

13

of possibility; they broke the Baron's head when he tried to defend her; the Baroness was cut to pieces; my poor pupil was treated exactly like his sister; and as to the castle, there is not one stone standing on another, not a barn, not a sheep, not a duck, not a tree; but we were well avenged, for the Abares did exactly the same to a neighbouring barony which belonged to a Bulgarian Lord."

At this, Candide swooned again; but, having recovered and having said all that he ought to say, he inquired the cause and effect, the sufficient reason which had reduced Pangloss to so piteous a state.

"Alas!" said Pangloss, "'tis love: love, the consoler of the human race, the preserver of the universe, the soul of all tender creatures, gentle love."

"Alas!" said Candide, "I am acquainted with this love, this sovereign of hearts, this soul of our soul; it has never brought me anything but one kiss and twenty kicks in the backside. How could this beautiful cause produce in you so abominable an effect?"

Pangloss replied as follows:

"My dear Candide! You remember Paquette, the maid-servant of our august Baroness; in her arms I enjoyed the delights of Paradise which have produced the tortures of Hell by which you see I am devoured; she was infected and perhaps is dead. Paquette received this present from a most learned monk, who had it from the source; for he received it from an old countess, who had it from a cavalry captain, who owed it to a marchioness, who derived it from a page, who had received it from a Jesuit, who, when a novice, had it in a direct line from one of the companions of Christopher Columbus. For my part, I shall not give it to anyone, for I am dying."

"O Pangloss!" exclaimed Candide, "this is a strange genealogy! Wasn't the devil at the root of it?"

"Not at all," replied that great man. "It was something indispensable in this best of worlds, a necessary ingredient; for, if Columbus in an island of America had not caught this disease, which poisons the source of generation, and often indeed prevents generation, we should not have chocolate and cochineal; it must also be noticed that hitherto in our continent this disease is peculiar to us, like theological disputes. The Turks, the Indians, the Persians, the Chinese, the Siamese and the Japanese are not yet familiar with it; but there is a sufficient reason why they in their turn should become familiar with it in a few centuries. Meanwhile, it has made marvellous progress among us, and especially in those large armies composed of honest, well-bred stipendiaries who decide the destiny of States; it may be asserted that when thirty thousand men fight a pitched battle against an equal number of troops, there are about twenty thousand with the pox on either side."

"Admirable!" said Candide. "But you must get cured."

"How can I?" said Pangloss. " I haven't a sou, my friend, and in the whole extent of this globe, you cannot be bled or receive an enema without paying or without someone paying for you."

This last speech determined Candide; he went and threw himself at the feet of his charitable Anabaptist, Jacques, and drew so touching a picture of the state to which his friend was reduced that the good easy man did not hesitate to succour Pangloss; he had him cured at his own expense. In this cure Pangloss only lost one eye and one ear. He could write well and knew arithmetic perfectly. The Anabaptist made him his bookkeeper. At the end of two months he was compelled to go to Lisbon on business and took his two philosophers on the boat with him. Pangloss explained to him how everything was for the best. Jacques was not of this opinion.

"Men," said he, "must have corrupted nature a little, for they were not born wolves, and they have become wolves. God did not give them twenty-four-pounder cannons or bayonets, and they have made bayonets and cannons to destroy each other. I might bring bankruptcies into the account and Justice which seizes the goods of bankrupts in order to deprive the creditors of them."

"It was all indispensable," replied the one-eyed doctor, "and private misfortunes make the public good, so that the more private misfortunes there are, the more everything is well."

While he was reasoning, the air grew dark, the winds blew from the four quarters of the globe and the ship was attacked by the most horrible tempest in sight of the port of Lisbon.

CHAPTER V

Storm, shipwreck, earthquake, and what happened to Dr Pangloss, to Candide and the Anabaptist Jacques

HALF the enfeebled passengers, suffering from that inconceivable anguish which the rolling of a ship causes in the nerves and in all the humours of bodies shaken in contrary directions, did not retain strength enough even to trouble about the danger. The other half screamed and prayed; the sails were torn, the masts broken, the vessel leaking. Those worked who could, no one co-operated, no one commanded. The Anabaptist tried to help the crew a little; he was on the main-deck; a furious sailor struck him violently and stretched him on the deck; but the blow he delivered gave him so violent a shock that he fell head-first out of the ship. He remained hanging and clinging to part of the broken mast. The good Jacques ran to his aid, helped him to climb back, and from the effort he made was flung into the sea in full view of the sailor, who allowed him to drown without condescending even to look at him. Candide came up, saw his benefactor reappear for a moment and then be engulfed for ever. He tried to throw himself after him into the sea; he was prevented by the philosopher Pangloss, who proved to him that the Lisbon roads had been expressly created for the Anabaptist to be drowned in them. While he was proving this *a priori*, the vessel sank, and every one

17

perished except Pangloss, Candide and the brutal sailor who had drowned the virtuous Anabaptist; the black-guard swam successfully to the shore and Pangloss and Candide were carried there on a plank.

When they had recovered a little, they walked to-ward Lisbon; they had a little money by the help of which they hoped to be saved from hunger after having escaped the storm.

Weeping the death of their benefactor, they had scarcely set foot in the town when they felt the earth tremble under their feet; the sea rose in foaming masses in the port and smashed the ships which rode at anchor. Whirlwinds of flame and ashes covered the streets and squares; the houses collapsed, the roofs were thrown upon the foundations, and the foundations were scat-tered; thirty thousand inhabitants of every age and both sexes were crushed under the ruins. Whistling and swearing, the sailor said:

"There'll be something to pick up here."

"What can be the sufficient reason for this phe-nomenon?" said Pangloss.

"It is the last day!" cried Candide.

The sailor immediately ran among the debris, dared death to find money, found it, seized it, got drunk, and having slept off his wine, purchased the favours of the first woman of good-will he met on the ruins of the houses and among the dead and dying. Pangloss, how-ever, pulled him by the sleeve.

"My friend," said he, "this is not well, you are dis-regarding universal reason, you choose the wrong time."

"Blood and 'ounds!" he retorted, "I am a sailor and I was born in Batavia; four times have I stamped on the crucifix during four voyages to Japan;[1] you have

---

[1]After a conspiracy of Christians in Japan, all foreigners were expelled. The Dutch, who had revealed the plot to the Emperor of Japan, alone were permitted to remain, on condition that they gave up all signs of Christianity and stamped on the crucifix.

found the right man for your universal reason!"

Candide had been hurt by some falling stones; he lay in the street covered with debris. He said to Pangloss:

"Alas! Get me a little wine and oil; I am dying."

"This earthquake is not a new thing," replied Pangloss. " The town of Lima felt the same shocks in America last year; similar causes produce similar effects; there must certainly be a train of sulphur underground from Lima to Lisbon."

"Nothing is more probable," replied Candide; "but, for God's sake, a little oil and wine."

"What do you mean, probable?" replied the philosopher; "I maintain that it is proved."

Candide lost consciousness, and Pangloss brought him a little water from a neighbouring fountain.

Next day they found a little food as they wandered among the ruins and regained a little strength. Afterwards they worked like others to help the inhabitants who had escaped death. Some citizens they had assisted gave them as good a dinner as could be expected in such a disaster; true, it was a dreary meal; the hosts watered their bread with their tears, but Pangloss consoled them by assuring them that things could not be otherwise.

"For," said he, "all this is for the best; for, if there is a volcano at Lisbon, it cannot be anywhere else; for it is impossible that things should not be where they are; for all is well."

A little, dark man, a familiar of the Inquisition, who sat beside him, politely took up the conversation, and said:

"Apparently you do not believe in original sin; for, if everything is for the best, there was neither fall nor punishment."

"I most humbly beg your excellency's pardon," replied Pangloss still more politely, "for the fall of man

19

and the curse necessarily entered into the best of all possible worlds."

"Then you do not believe in free-will?" said the familiar.

"Your excellency will pardon me," said Pangloss; "free-will can exist with absolute necessity; for it was necessary that we should be free; for in short, limited will . . ."

Pangloss was in the middle of his phrase when the familiar nodded to his armed attendant who was pouring out port or Oporto wine for him.

$\mathcal{H}$ ow a splendid auto-da-fé was held to prevent earthquakes, and how Candide was flogged

AFTER the earthquake which destroyed three-quarters of Lisbon, the wise men of that country could discover no more efficacious way of preventing a total ruin than by giving the people a splendid *auto-da-fé*. It was decided by the university of Coimbra that the sight of several persons being slowly burned in great ceremony is an infallible secret for preventing earthquakes.

Consequently they had arrested a Biscayan convicted of having married his fellow-godmother, and two Portuguese who, when eating a chicken, had thrown away the bacon; after dinner they came and bound Dr Pangloss and his disciple Candide, one because he had spoken and the other because he had listened with an air of approbation; they were both carried separately to extremely cool apartments, where there was never any discomfort from the sun; a week afterwards each was dressed in a sanbenito and their heads were ornamented with paper mitres; Candide's mitre and sanbenito were painted with flames upside down and with devils who had neither tails nor claws; but Pangloss's devils had claws and tails, and his flames were upright.

Dressed in this manner they marched in procession and listened to a most pathetic sermon, followed by lovely plain-song music. Candide was flogged in time to the music, while the singing went on: the Biscayan and the two men who had not wanted to eat bacon

21

were burned, and Pangloss was hanged, although this
is not the custom. The very same day, the earth shook
again with a terrible clamour.

Candide, terrified, dumbfounded, bewildered and

covered with blood, quivering from head to foot, said
to himself:

"If this is the best of all possible worlds, what are
the others? Let it pass that I was flogged, for I was
flogged by the Bulgarians, but, O my dear Pangloss!
The greatest of philosophers! Must I see you hanged

without knowing why! O my dear Anabaptist! The best of men! Was it necessary that you should be drowned in port! O Miss Cunegonde! The pearl of women! Was it necessary that your belly should be slit!"

He was returning, scarcely able to support himself, preached at, flogged, absolved and blessed, when an old woman accosted him and said:

"Courage, my son, follow me."

CHAPTER VII

==

How an old woman took care of Candide and how he regained that which he loved

==

CANDIDE did not take courage, but he followed the old woman to a hovel; she gave him a pot of ointment to rub on, and left him food and drink; she pointed out a fairly clean bed; near the bed there was a suit of clothes.

"Eat, drink, sleep," said she, "and may our Lady of Atocha, my Lord Saint Anthony of Padua and my Lord Saint James of Compostella take care of you; I shall come back to-morrow."

Candide, still amazed by all he had seen, by all he had suffered, and still more by the old woman's charity, tried to kiss her hand.

" 'Tis not my hand you should kiss," said the old woman, "I shall come back to-morrow. Rub on the ointment, eat and sleep."

In spite of all his misfortune, Candide ate and went to sleep. Next day the old woman brought him breakfast, examined his back and smeared him with another ointment; later she brought him dinner, and returned in the evening with supper. The next day she went through the same ceremony.

"Who are you?" Candide kept asking her. "Who has inspired you with so much kindness? How can I thank you?"

The good woman never made any reply; she returned in the evening without any supper.

"Come with me," she said, "and do not speak a word."

24

She took him by the arm and walked into the country with him for about a quarter of a mile; they came to an isolated house, surrounded with gardens and canals. The old woman knocked at a little door. It was opened; she led Candide up a back stairway into a gilded apartment, left him on a brocaded sofa, shut the door and went away. Candide thought he was dreaming, and felt that his whole life was a bad dream and the present moment an agreeable dream.

The old woman soon reappeared; she was supporting with some difficulty a trembling woman of majestic stature, glittering with precious stones and covered with a veil.

"Remove the veil," said the old woman to Candide. The young man advanced and lifted the veil with a timid hand. What a moment! What a surprise! He thought he saw Miss Cunegonde, in fact he was looking at her, it was she herself. His strength failed him, he could not utter a word and fell at her feet. Cunegonde fell on the sofa. The old woman dosed them with distilled waters; they recovered their senses and began to speak: at first they uttered only broken words, questions and answers at cross purposes, sighs, tears, exclamations. The old woman advised them to make less noise and left them alone.

"What! Is it you?" said Candide. "You are alive, and I find you here in Portugal! Then you were not raped? Your belly was not slit, as the philosopher Pangloss assured me?"

"Yes, indeed," said the fair Cunegonde; "but those two accidents are not always fatal."

"But your father and mother were killed?"

" 'Tis only too true," said Cunegonde, weeping.

"And your brother?"

"My brother was killed too."

"And why are you in Portugal? And how did you know I was here? And by what strange adventure have you brought me to this house?"

"I will tell you everything," replied the lady, "but first of all you must tell me everything that has happened to you since the innocent kiss you gave me and the kicks you received."

Candide obeyed with profound respect; and, although he was bewildered, although his voice was weak and trembling, although his back was still a little painful, he related in the most natural manner all he had endured since the moment of their separation. Cunegonde raised her eyes to Heaven; she shed tears at the death of the good Anabaptist and Pangloss, after which she spoke as follows to Candide, who did not miss a word and devoured her with his eyes.

CHAPTER VIII

Cunegonde's Story

"I WAS fast asleep in bed when it pleased Heaven to send the Bulgarians to our noble castle of Thunder-ten-tronckh; they murdered my father and brother and cut my mother to pieces. A large Bulgarian six feet tall, seeing that I had swooned at the spectacle, began to rape me; this brought me to, I recovered my senses, I screamed, I struggled, I bit, I scratched, I tried to tear out the big Bulgarian's eyes, not knowing that what was happening in my father's castle was a matter of custom; the brute stabbed me with a knife in the left side where I still have the scar."

"Alas! I hope I shall see it," said the naïf Candide.

"You shall see it," said Cunegonde, "but let me go on."

"Go on," said Candide.

She took up the thread of her story as follows:

"A Bulgarian captain came in, saw me covered with blood, and the soldier did not disturb himself. The captain was angry at the brute's lack of respect to him, and killed him on my body. Afterwards, he had me bandaged and took me to his billet as a prisoner of war. I washed the few shirts he had and did the cooking; I must admit he thought me very pretty; and I will not deny that he was very well built and that his skin was white and soft; otherwise he had little wit and little philosophy; it was plain that he had not been brought up by Dr Pangloss. At the end of three months he lost all his money and got tired of me; he sold me to a Jew named Don Issachar, who traded in Holland and Portugal and had a passion for women. This Jew

27

devoted himself to my person, but he could not triumph over it; I resisted him better than the Bulgarian soldier; a lady of honour may be raped once, but it strengthens her virtue. In order to subdue me, the Jew brought me to this country house. Up till then I believed that there was nothing on earth so splendid as the castle of Thunder-ten-tronckh; I was undeceived.

"One day the Grand Inquisitor noticed me at Mass; he ogled me continually and sent a message that he wished to speak to me on secret affairs. I was taken to his palace; I informed him of my birth; he pointed out how much it was beneath my rank to belong to an Israelite. A proposition was made on his behalf to Don Issachar to give me up to His Lordship. Don Issachar, who is the court banker and a man of influence, would not agree. The Inquisitor threatened him with an *auto-da-fé*. At last the Jew was frightened and made a bargain whereby the house and I belong to both in common. The Jew has Mondays, Wednesdays and the Sabbath day, and the Inquisitor has the other days of the week. This arrangement has lasted for six months. It has not been without quarrels; for it has often been debated whether the night between Saturday and Sunday belonged to the old law or the new. For my part, I have hitherto resisted them both; and I think that is the reason why they still love me.

"At last My Lord the Inquisitor was pleased to arrange an *auto-da-fé* to remove the scourge of earthquakes and to intimidate Don Issachar. He honoured me with an invitation. I had an excellent seat; and refreshments were served to the ladies between the Mass and the execution. I was indeed horror-stricken when I saw the burning of the two Jews and the honest Biscayan who had married his fellow-godmother; but what was my surprise, my terror, my anguish, when I saw in a sanbenito and under a mitre a face which

resembled Pangloss's! I rubbed my eyes, I looked carefully, I saw him hanged; and I fainted. I had scarcely
recovered my senses when I saw you stripped naked;
that was the height of horror, of consternation, of grief
and despair. I will frankly tell you that your skin is
even whiter and of a more perfect tint than that of my
Bulgarian captain. This spectacle redoubled all the
feelings which crushed and devoured me. I exclaimed,
I tried to say: 'Stop, barbarians!' but my voice failed
and my cries would have been useless. When you had
been well flogged, I said to myself: 'How does it happen that the charming Candide and the wise Pangloss
are in Lisbon, the one to receive a hundred lashes, and
the other to be hanged, by order of My Lord the Inquisitor, whose darling I am? Pangloss deceived me
cruelly when he said that all is for the best in the
world.'

"I was agitated, distracted, sometimes beside myself
and sometimes ready to die of faintness, and my head
was filled with the massacre of my father, of my mother,
of my brother, the insolence of my horrid Bulgarian
soldier, the gash he gave me, my slavery, my life as a
kitchen-wench, my Bulgarian captain, my horrid Don
Issachar, my abominable Inquisitor, the hanging of
Dr Pangloss, that long plain-song *miserere* during which
you were flogged, and above all the kiss I gave you
behind the screen that day when I saw you for the last
time. I praised God for bringing you back to me through
so many trials, I ordered my old woman to take care of
you and to bring you here as soon as she could. She has
carried out my commission very well; I have enjoyed
the inexpressible pleasure of seeing you again, of listen-
ing to you, and of speaking to you. You must be very
hungry; I have a good appetite; let us begin by having
supper."

Both sat down to supper; and after supper they

returned to the handsome sofa we have already mentioned; they were still there when Signor Don Issachar,
one of the masters of the house, arrived. It was the
day of the Sabbath. He came to enjoy his rights and to
express his tender love.

CHAPTER IX

What happened to Cunegonde, to Candide, to the Grand Inquisitor and to a Jew

THIS Issachar was the most choleric Hebrew who had been seen in Israel since the Babylonian captivity.

"What!" said he. "Bitch of a Galilean, isn't it enough to have the Inquisitor? Must this scoundrel share with me too?"

So saying, he drew a long dagger which he always carried and, thinking that his adversary was unarmed, threw himself upon Candide; but our good Westphalian had received an excellent sword from the old woman along with his suit of clothes. He drew his sword, and although he had a most gentle character, laid the Israelite stone-dead on the floor at the feet of the fair Cunegonde.

"Holy Virgin!" she exclaimed, "what will become of us? A man killed in my house! If the police come we are lost."

"If Pangloss had not been hanged," said Candide, "he would have given us good advice in this extremity, for he was a great philosopher. In default of him, let us consult the old woman."

She was extremely prudent and was beginning to give her advice when another little door opened. It was an hour after midnight, and Sunday was beginning.

This day belonged to My Lord the Inquisitor. He came in and saw the flogged Candide sword in hand, a corpse lying on the ground, Cunegonde in terror, and the old woman giving advice.

At this moment, here is what happened in Candide's soul and the manner of his reasoning:

"If this holy man calls for help, he will infallibly have me burned; he might do as much to Cunegonde; he had me pitilessly lashed; he is my rival; I am in the mood to kill, there is no room for hesitation."

His reasoning was clear and swift; and, without giving the Inquisitor time to recover from his surprise, he pierced him through and through and cast him beside the Jew.

"Here's another," said Cunegonde, "there is no chance of mercy; we are excommunicated, our last hour has come. How does it happen that you, who were born so mild, should kill a Jew and a prelate in two minutes?"

"My dear young lady," replied Candide, "when a man is in love, jealous, and has been flogged by the Inquisition, he is beside himself."

The old woman then spoke up and said:

"In the stable are three Andalusian horses, with their saddles and bridles; let the brave Candide prepare them; madam has moidores and diamonds; let us mount quickly, although I can only sit on one buttock, and go to Cadiz; the weather is beautifully fine, and it is most pleasant to travel in the coolness of the night."

Candide immediately saddled the three horses. Cunegonde, the old woman and he rode thirty miles without stopping.

While they were riding away, the Holy Brotherhood arrived at the house; My Lord was buried in a splendid church and Issachar was thrown into a sewer.

Candide, Cunegonde and the old woman had already reached the little town of Avacena in the midst of the mountains of the Sierra Morena; and they talked in their inn as follows.

CHAPTER X

How Candide, Cunegonde and the old woman arrived at Cadiz in great distress, and how they embarked

"WHO can have stolen my pistoles and my diamonds?" said Cunegonde, weeping. "How shall we live? What shall we do? Where shall we find Inquisitors and Jews to give me others?"

"Alas!" said the old woman, "I strongly suspect a reverend Franciscan father who slept last night in the same inn at Badajoz with us; Heaven forbid that I should judge rashly! But he twice came into our room and left long before we did."

"Alas!" said Candide, "the good Pangloss often proved to me that this world's goods are common to all men and that every one has an equal right to them. According to these principles the monk should have left us enough to continue our journey. Have you nothing left then, my fair Cunegonde?"

"Not a maravedi," said she.

"What are we to do?" said Candide.

"Sell one of the horses," said the old woman. "I will ride postillion behind Miss Cunegonde, although I can only sit on one buttock, and we will get to Cadiz."

In the same hotel there was a Benedictine prior. He bought the horse very cheap. Candide, Cunegonde and the old woman passed through Lucena, Chillas, Lebrixa, and at last reached Cadiz. A fleet was there being equipped and troops were being raised to bring to reason the reverend Jesuit fathers of Paraguay, who were accused of causing the revolt of one of their tribes against the kings of Spain and Portugal near the town of Sacramento. Candide, having served with the Bulgarians, went through the Bulgarian drill before the general of the little army with so much grace, celerity, skill, pride and agility, that he was given the command of an infantry company. He was now a captain; he embarked with Miss Cunegonde, the old woman, two servants, and the two Andalusian horses which had belonged to the Grand Inquisitor of Portugal.

During the voyage they had many discussions about the philosophy of poor Pangloss.

"We are going to a new world," said Candide, "and no doubt it is there that everything is for the best; for it must be admitted that one might lament a little over the physical and moral happenings in our own world."

"I love you with all my heart," said Cunegonde, "but my soul is still shocked by what I have seen and undergone."

"All will be well," replied Candide; "the sea in this new world already is better than the seas of our Europe; it is calmer and the winds are more constant. It is certainly the new world which is the best of all possible worlds."

"God grant it!" said Cunegonde, "but I have been so horribly unhappy in mine that my heart is nearly closed to hope."

"You complain," said the old woman to them. "Alas! you have not endured such misfortunes as mine."

Cunegonde almost laughed and thought it most amusing of the old woman to assert that she was more unfortunate.

"Alas! my dear," said she, "unless you have been raped by two Bulgarians, stabbed twice in the belly, have had two castles destroyed, two fathers and mothers murdered before your eyes, and have seen two of your lovers flogged in an *auto-da-fé*, I do not see how you can surpass me; moreover, I was born a Baroness with seventy-two quarterings and I have been a kitchen-wench."

"You do not know my birth," said the old woman, "and if I showed you my backside you would not talk as you do and you would suspend your judgment."

This speech aroused intense curiosity in the minds of Cunegonde and Candide. And the old woman spoke as follows.

CHAPTER XI

The old woman's story

"My eyes were not always bloodshot and red-rimmed; my nose did not always touch my chin and I was not always a servant. I am the daughter of Pope Urban X and the Princess of Palestrina.[1] Until I was fourteen I was brought up in a palace to which all the castles of your German Barons would not have served as stables; and one of my dresses cost more than all the magnificence of Westphalia. I increased in beauty, in grace, in talents, among pleasures, respect and hopes; already I inspired love, my breasts were forming; and what breasts! White, firm, carved like those of the Venus de' Medici. And what eyes! What eyelids! What black eyebrows! What fire shone from my two eyeballs, and dimmed the glitter of the stars, as the local poets pointed out to me. The women who dressed and undressed me fell into ecstasy when they beheld me in front and behind; and all the men would have liked to be in their place.

"I was betrothed to a ruling prince of Massa-Carrara. What a prince! As beautiful as I was, formed of gentleness and charms, brilliantly witty and burning with love; I loved him with a first love, idolatrously and extravagantly. The marriage ceremonies were arranged with unheard-of pomp and magnificence; there were continual fêtes, revels and comic operas; all Italy wrote sonnets for me and not a good one among them.

---

[1] A posthumously printed note of Voltaire's on this passage runs as follows: "Notice the author's extreme discretion; up till now there has never been any Pope called Urban X; he shrank from giving a bastard to a known Pope. What circumspection! What conscientious delicacy!"

"I touched the moment of my happiness when an old marchioness who had been my prince's mistress invited him to take chocolate with her; less than two hours afterwards he died in horrible convulsions; but that is only a trifle. My mother was in despair, though less distressed than I, and wished to absent herself for a time from a place so disastrous. She had a most beautiful estate near Gaeta; we embarked on a galley, gilded like the altar of St Peter's at Rome. A Salle pirate swooped down and boarded us; our soldiers defended us like soldiers of the Pope; they threw down their arms, fell on their knees and asked the pirates for absolution *in articulo mortis*.

"They were immediately stripped as naked as monkeys, and my mother, our ladies of honour and myself as well. The diligence with which these gentlemen strip people is truly admirable; but I was still more surprised by their inserting a finger in a place belonging to all of us where we women usually only allow the end of a syringe. This appeared to me a very strange ceremony; but that is how we judge everything when we leave our own country. I soon learned that it was to find out if we had hidden any diamonds there; 'tis a custom established from time immemorial among the civilised nations who roam the seas. I have learned that the religious Knights of Malta never fail in it when they capture Turks and Turkish women; this is an international law which has never been broken.

"I will not tell you how hard it is for a young princess to be taken with her mother as a slave to Morocco; you will also guess all we had to endure in the pirates' ship. My mother was still very beautiful; our ladies of honour, even our waiting-maids possessed more charms than could be found in all Africa; and I was ravishing, I was beauty, grace itself, and I was a virgin; I did not remain so long; the flower which had been reserved for the handsome prince of Massa-Carrara was ravished from me by a pirate captain; he was an abominable negro who thought he was doing me a great honour. The Princess of Palestrina and I must indeed have been strong to bear up against all we endured before our arrival in Morocco! But let that pass; these things are so common that they are not worth mentioning.

"Morocco was swimming in blood when we arrived. The fifty sons of the Emperor Muley Ismael had each a faction; and this produced fifty civil wars, of blacks against blacks, blacks against browns, browns against browns, mulattoes against mulattoes. There was continual carnage throughout the whole extent of the empire.

"Scarcely had we landed when the blacks of a party hostile to that of my pirate arrived with the purpose of depriving him of his booty. After the diamonds and the gold, we were the most valuable possessions. I witnessed a fight such as is never seen in your European climates. The blood of the northern peoples is not sufficiently ardent; their madness for women does not reach the point which is common in Africa. The Europeans seem to have milk in their veins; but vitriol and fire flow in the veins of the inhabitants of Mount Atlas and the neighbouring countries. They fought with the fury of the lions, tigers and serpents of the country to determine who should have us. A Moor grasped my mother by the right arm, my captain's lieutenant held her by the left arm; a Moorish soldier held one leg and one of our pirates seized the other. In a moment nearly all our women were seized in the same way by four soldiers. My captain kept me hidden behind him; he had a scimitar in his hand and killed everybody who opposed his fury. I saw my mother and all our Italian women torn in pieces, gashed, massacred by the monsters who disputed them. The prisoners, my companions, those who had captured them, soldiers, sailors, blacks, browns, whites, mulattoes and finally my captain were all killed and I remained expiring on a heap of corpses. As every one knows, such scenes go on in an area of more than three hundred square leagues and yet no one ever fails to recite the five daily prayers ordered by Mahomet.

"With great difficulty I extricated myself from the bloody heaps of corpses and dragged myself to the foot of a large orange-tree on the bank of a stream; there I fell down with terror, weariness, horror, despair and hunger. Soon afterwards, my exhausted senses fell into a sleep which was more like a swoon than repose. I was in this state of weakness and insensibility between life and death when I felt myself oppressed by something which moved on my body. I opened my eyes and saw a white man of good appearance who was sighing and muttering between his teeth: *O che sciagura d'essere senza coglioni!*

CHAPTER XII

Continuation of the old woman's misfortunes

"Amazed and delighted to hear my native language, and not less surprised at the words spoken by this man, I replied that there were greater misfortunes than that of which he complained. In a few words I informed him of the horrors I had undergone and then swooned again. He carried me to a neighbouring house, had me put to bed, gave me food, waited on me, consoled me, flattered me, told me he had never seen anyone so beautiful as I, and that he had never so much regretted that which no one could give back to him.

" 'I was born at Naples,' he said, 'and every year they make two or three thousand children there into capons; some die of it, others acquire voices more beautiful than women's, and others become the governors of States. This operation was performed upon me with very great success and I was a musician in the chapel of the Princess of Palestrina.'

" 'Of my mother,' I exclaimed.

" 'Of your mother!' cried he, weeping. 'What! Are you that young princess I brought up to the age of six and who even then gave promise of being as beautiful as you are?'

" 'I am! my mother is four hundred yards from here, cut into quarters under a heap of corpses. . . .'

"I related all that had happened to me; he also told me his adventures and informed me how he had been sent to the King of Morocco by a Christian power to make a treaty with that monarch whereby he was supplied with powder, cannons and ships to help to exterminate the commerce of other Christians.

" 'My mission is accomplished,' said this honest eunuch, 'I am about to embark at Ceuta and I will take you back to Italy. *Ma che sciagura d'essere senza coglioni!*'

"I thanked him with tears of gratitude; and instead of taking me back to Italy he conducted me to Algiers and sold me to the Dey. I had scarcely been sold when the plague, which had gone through Africa, Asia and Europe, broke out furiously in Algiers. You have seen earthquakes; but have you ever seen the plague?"

"Never," replied the Baroness.

"If you had," replied the old woman, "you would admit that it is much worse than an earthquake. It is very common in Africa; I caught it. Imagine the situation of a Pope's daughter aged fifteen, who in three months had undergone poverty and slavery, had been raped nearly every day, had seen her mother cut into four pieces, had undergone hunger and war, and was now dying of the plague in Algiers. However, I did not die; but my eunuch and the Dey and almost all the seraglio of Algiers perished.

"When the first ravages of this frightful plague were over, the Dey's slaves were sold. A merchant bought me and carried me to Tunis; he sold me to another merchant who re-sold me at Tripoli; from Tripoli I was re-sold to Alexandria, from Alexandria re-sold to Smyrna, from Smyrna to Constantinople. I was finally bought by an Aga of the Janizaries, who was soon ordered to defend Azov against the Russians who were besieging it.

"The Aga, who was a man of great gallantry, took his whole seraglio with him, and lodged us in a little fort on the Islands of Palus-Maeotis, guarded by two black eunuchs and twenty soldiers. He killed a prodigious number of Russians, but they returned the compliment as well. Azov was given up to fire and blood, neither sex nor age was pardoned; only our little fort remained; and the enemy tried to reduce it by starving us. The twenty Janizaries had sworn never to surrender. The extremities of hunger to which they were reduced forced them to eat our two eunuchs for fear of breaking their oath. Some days later they resolved to eat the women.

"We had with us a most pious and compassionate Imam who delivered a fine sermon to them by which he persuaded them not to kill us altogether.

" 'Cut,' said he, 'only one buttock from each of these ladies and you will make very good cheer; if you have to return, there will still be as much left in a few days; Heaven will be pleased at so charitable an action and you will be saved.'

"He was very eloquent and persuaded them. This horrible operation was performed upon us; the Imam anointed us with the same balm that is used for children who have just been circumcised; we were all at the point of death.

"Scarcely had the Janizaries finished the meal we had supplied when the Russians arrived in flat-bottomed boats; not a Janizary escaped. The Russians paid no attention to the state we were in. There are French doctors everywhere; one of them, who was very skilful, took care of us; he healed us and I shall remember all my life that, when my wounds were cured, he made propositions to me. For the rest, he told us all to cheer up; he told us that the same thing had happened in several sieges and that it was a law of war.

"As soon as my companions could walk they were sent to Moscow. I fell to the lot of a Boyar who made me his gardener and gave me twenty lashes a day. But at the end of two years this lord was broken on the

43

wheel with thirty other Boyars owing to some court disturbance, and I profited by this adventure; I fled; I crossed all Russia; for a long time I was servant in an inn at Riga, then at Rostock, at Wismar, at Leipzig, at Cassel, at Utrecht, at Leyden, at the Hague, at Rotterdam; I have grown old in misery and in shame, with only half a backside, always remembering that I was the daughter of a Pope; a hundred times I wanted to kill myself but I still loved life. This ridiculous weakness is perhaps the most disastrous of our inclinations; for is there anything sillier than to desire to bear continually a burden one always wishes to throw on the ground; to look upon oneself with horror and yet to cling to oneself; in short, to caress the serpent which devours us until he has eaten our heart?

"In the countries it has been my fate to traverse and in the inns where I have served I have seen a prodigious number of people who hated their lives; but I have only seen twelve who voluntarily put an end to their misery: three negroes, four Englishmen, four Genevans and a German professor named Robeck. I ended up as servant to the Jew, Don Issachar; he placed me in your service, my fair young lady; I attached myself to your fate and have been more occupied with your adventures than with my own. I should never even have spoken of my misfortunes, if you had not piqued me a little and if it had not been the custom on board ship to tell stories to pass the time. In short, Miss, I have had experience, I know the world; provide yourself with an entertainment, make each passenger tell you his story; and if there is one who has not often cursed his life, who has not often said to himself that he was the most unfortunate of men, throw me head-first into the sea."

CHAPTER XIII

How Candide was obliged to separate from the fair Cunegonde and the old woman

THE fair Cunegonde, having heard the old woman's story, treated her with all the politeness due to a person of her rank and merit. She accepted the proposition and persuaded all the passengers one after the other to tell her their adventures. She and Candide admitted that the old woman was right.

"It was most unfortunate," said Candide, "that the wise Pangloss was hanged contrary to custom at an *auto-da-fé;* he would have said admirable things about the physical and moral evils which cover the earth and the sea, and I should feel myself strong enough to urge a few objections with all due respect."

While each of the passengers was telling his story the ship proceeded on its way. They arrived at Buenos Ayres. Cunegonde, Captain Candide and the old woman went to call on the governor, Don Fernando d'Ibaraa y Figueora y Mascarenes y Lampourdos y Souza. This gentleman had the pride befitting a man who owned so many names. He talked to men with a most noble disdain, turning his nose up so far, raising his voice so pitilessly, assuming so imposing a tone, affecting so lofty a carriage, that all who addressed him were tempted to give him a thrashing. He had a furious passion for women. Cunegonde seemed to him the most beautiful woman he had ever seen. The first thing he did was to ask if she were the Captain's wife. The air with

which he asked this question alarmed Candide; he
did not dare say that she was his wife, because as a
matter of fact she was not; he dared not say she was his
sister, because she was not that either; and although
this official lie was formerly extremely fashionable
among the ancients, and might be useful to the moderns,
his soul was too pure to depart from truth.

"Miss Cunegonde," said he, "is about to do me the
honour of marrying me, and we beg your excellency to
be present at the wedding."

Don Fernando d'Ibaraa y Figueora y Mascarenes y
Lampourdos y Souza twisted his moustache, smiled
bitterly and ordered Captain Candide to go and inspect
his company. Candide obeyed; the governor remained
with Miss Cunegonde. He declared his passion, vowed
that the next day he would marry her publicly, or otherwise, as it might please her charms. Cunegonde asked
for a quarter of an hour to collect herself, to consult
the old woman and to make up her mind.

The old woman said to Cunegonde:

"You have seventy-two quarterings and you haven't
a shilling; it is in your power to be the wife of the
greatest Lord in South America, who has an exceed-
ingly fine moustache; is it for you to pride yourself on a
rigid fidelity? You have been raped by Bulgarians; a
Jew and an Inquisitor have enjoyed your good graces;
misfortunes confer certain rights. If I were in your
place, I confess I should not have the least scruple
in marrying the governor and making Captain Candide's fortune."

While the old woman was speaking with all that
prudence which comes from age and experience, they
saw a small ship come into the harbour; an Alcayde and
some Alguazils were on board, and this is what had
happened.

The old woman had guessed correctly that it was a

long-sleeved Franciscan who stole Cunegonde's money and jewels at Badajoz, when she was flying in all haste with Candide. The monk tried to sell some of the gems to a jeweller. The merchant recognised them as the property of the Grand Inquisitor. Before the monk was hanged he confessed that he had stolen them; he described the persons and the direction they were taking. The flight of Cunegonde and Candide was already known. They were followed to Cadiz; without any waste of time a vessel was sent in pursuit of them. The vessel was already in the harbour at Buenos Ayres. The rumour spread that an Alcayde was about to land and that he was in pursuit of the murderers of His Lordship the Grand Inquisitor. The prudent old woman saw in a moment what was to be done.

"You cannot escape," she said to Cunegonde, "and you have nothing to fear; you did not kill His Lordship; moreover, the governor is in love with you and will not allow you to be maltreated; stay here."

She ran to Candide at once.

"Fly," said she, "or in an hour's time you will be burned."

There was not a moment to lose; but how could he leave Cunegonde and where could he take refuge?

CHAPTER XIV

How Candide and Cacambo were received by the Jesuits in Paraguay

CANDIDE had brought from Cadiz a valet of a sort which is very common on the coasts of Spain and in the colonies. He was one-quarter Spanish, the child of a half-breed in Tucuman; he had been a choir-boy, a sacristan, a sailor, a monk, a postman, a soldier and a lackey. His name was Cacambo, and he loved his master because his master was a very good man. He saddled the two Andalusian horses with all speed.

"Come, master, we must follow the old woman's advice; let us be off and ride without looking behind us."

Candide shed tears.

"O my dear Cunegonde! Must I abandon you just when the governor was about to marry us! Cunegonde, brought here from such a distant land, what will become of you?"

"She will become what she can," said Cacambo. "Women never trouble about themselves; God will see to her; let us be off."

"Where are you taking me? Where are we going? What shall we do without Cunegonde?" said Candide.

"By St James of Compostella," said Cacambo, "you were going to fight the Jesuits; let us go and fight for them; I know the roads, I will take you to their kingdom, they will be charmed to have a Captain who can drill in the Bulgarian fashion; you will make a prodigious fortune; when a man fails in one world, he

48

succeeds in another. 'Tis a very great pleasure to see and do new things.''

"Then you have been in Paraguay?" said Candide.

"Yes, indeed," said Cacambo. "I was servitor in the College of the Assumption, and I know the government of *Los Padres* as well as I know the streets of Cadiz. Their government is a most admirable thing. The kingdom is already more than three hundred leagues in diameter and is divided into thirty provinces. *Los Padres* have everything and the people have nothing; 'tis the masterpiece of reason and justice. For my part, I know nothing so divine as *Los Padres* who here make war on the Kings of Spain and Portugal and in Europe act as their confessors; who here kill Spaniards and at Madrid send them to Heaven; all this delights me; come on; you will be the happiest of men. What a pleasure it will be to *Los Padres* when they know there is coming to them a captain who can drill in the Bulgarian manner!"

As soon as they reached the first barrier, Cacambo told the picket that a captain wished to speak to the Commandant. This information was carried to the main guard. A Paraguayan officer ran to the feet of the Commandant to tell him the news. Candide and Cacambo were disarmed and their two Andalusian horses were taken from them. The two strangers were brought in between two ranks of soldiers; the Commandant was at the end, with a three-cornered hat on his head, his gown tucked up, a sword at his side and a spontoon in his hand. He made a sign and immediately the two new-comers were surrounded by twenty-four soldiers. A sergeant told them that they must wait, that the Commandant could not speak to them, that the reverend father provincial did not allow any Spaniard to open his mouth in his presence or to remain more than three hours in the country.

"And where is the reverend father provincial?" said Cacambo.

"He is on parade after having said Mass, and you will have to wait three hours before you will be allowed to kiss his spurs."

"But," said Cacambo, "the captain, who is dying of hunger just as I am, is not a Spaniard but a German; can we not break our fast while we are waiting for his reverence?"

The sergeant went at once to inform the Commandant of this.

"Blessed be God!" said that lord. "Since he is a German I can speak to him; bring him to my arbour."

Candide was immediately taken to a leafy summer-house decorated with a very pretty colonnade of green and gold marble, and lattices enclosing parrots, humming-birds, colibris, guinea-hens and many other rare birds. An excellent breakfast stood ready in gold dishes; and while the Paraguayans were eating maize from wooden bowls, out of doors and in the heat of the sun, the reverend father Commandant entered the arbour.

He was a very handsome young man, with a full face, a fairly white skin, red cheeks, arched eyebrows, keen eyes, red ears, vermilion lips, a haughty air, but a haughtiness which was neither that of a Spaniard nor of a Jesuit. Candide and Cacambo were given back the arms which had been taken from them and their two Andalusian horses; Cacambo fed them with oats near the arbour, and kept his eye on them for fear of a surprise.

Candide first kissed the hem of the Commandant's gown and then they sat down to table.

"So you are a German?" said the Jesuit in that language.

"Yes, reverend father," said Candide.

As they spoke these words they gazed at each other with extreme surprise and an emotion they could not control.

"And what part of Germany do you come from?" said the Jesuit.

"From the filthy province of Westphalia," said Candide; "I was born in the castle of Thunder-ten-tronckh."

"Heavens! Is it possible!" cried the Commandant.

"What a miracle!" cried Candide.

"Can it be you?" said the Commandant.

" 'Tis impossible!" said Candide.

They both fell over backwards, embraced and shed rivers of tears.

"What! Can it be you, reverend father? You, the fair Cunegonde's brother! You, who were killed by the Bulgarians! You, the son of My Lord the Baron! You, a Jesuit in Paraguay! The world is indeed a strange place! O Pangloss! Pangloss! How happy you would have been if you had not been hanged!"

The Commandant sent away the negro slaves and the Paraguayans who were serving wine in goblets of rock-crystal. A thousand times did he thank God and

St Ignatius; he clasped Candide in his arms; their faces were wet with tears.

"You would be still more surprised, more touched, more beside yourself," said Candide, "if I were to tell you that Miss Cunegonde, your sister, whom you thought disembowelled, is in the best of health."

"Where?"

"In your neighbourhood, with the governor of Buenos Ayres; and I came to make war on you."

Every word they spoke in this long conversation piled marvel on marvel. Their whole souls flew from their tongues, listened in their ears and sparkled in their eyes. As they were Germans, they sat at table for a long time, waiting for the reverend father provincial; and the Commandant spoke as follows to his dear Candide.

CHAPTER XV

How Candide killed his dear Cunegonde's brother

"I SHALL remember all my life the horrible day when I saw my father and mother killed and my sister raped. When the Bulgarians had gone, my adorable sister could not be found, and my mother, my father and I, two maid-servants and three little murdered boys were placed in a cart to be buried in a Jesuit chapel two leagues from the castle of my fathers. A Jesuit sprinkled us with holy water; it was horribly salt; a few drops fell in my eyes; the father noticed that my eyelid trembled, he put his hand on my heart and felt that it was still beating; I was attended to and at the end of three weeks was as well as if nothing had happened. You know, my dear Candide, that I was a very pretty youth, and I became still prettier; and so the Reverend Father Croust, the Superior of the house, was inspired with a most tender friendship for me; he gave me the dress of a novice and some time afterwards I was sent to Rome. The Father General wished to recruit some young German Jesuits. The sovereigns of Paraguay take as few Spanish Jesuits as they can; they prefer foreigners, whom they think they can control better. The Reverend Father General thought me apt to labour in his vineyard. I set off with a Pole and a Tyrolese. When I arrived I was honoured with the subdeaconship and a lieutenancy; I am now colonel and priest. We shall give the King of Spain's troops a warm reception; I guarantee they will be excommunicated and beaten. Providence has sent you here to help us. But is it really true that my dear sister Cunegonde is in the neighbourhood with the governor of Buenos Ayres?"

Candide assured him on oath that nothing could be truer. Their tears began to flow once more.

The Baron seemed never to grow tired of embracing Candide; he called him his brother, his saviour.

"Ah! My dear Candide," said he, "perhaps we shall enter the town together as conquerors and regain my sister Cunegonde."

"I desire it above all things," said Candide, "for I meant to marry her and I still hope to do so."

"You, insolent wretch!" replied the Baron. "Would you have the impudence to marry my sister who has seventy-two quarterings! I consider you extremely impudent to dare to speak to me of such a fool-hardy intention!"

Candide, petrified at this speech, replied:

"Reverend Father, all the quarterings in the world are of no importance; I rescued your sister from the arms of a Jew and an Inquisitor; she is under considerable obligation to me and wishes to marry me. Dr Pangloss always said that men are equal and I shall certainly marry her."

"We shall see about that, scoundrel!" said the Jesuit Baron of Thunder-ten-tronckh, at the same time hitting him violently in the face with the flat of his sword. Candide promptly drew his own and stuck it up to the hilt in the Jesuit Baron's belly; but, as he drew it forth smoking, he began to weep.

"Alas! My God," said he, "I have killed my old master, my friend, my brother-in-law; I am the mildest man in the world and I have already killed three men, two of them priests."

Cacambo, who was acting as sentry at the door of the arbour, ran in.

"There is nothing left for us but to sell our lives

dearly," said his master. "Somebody will certainly come into the arbour and we must die weapon in hand."

Cacambo, who had seen this sort of thing before, did not lose his head; he took off the Baron's Jesuit gown, put it on Candide, gave him the dead man's square bonnet, and made him mount a horse. All this was done in the twinkling of an eye.

"Let us gallop, master; every one will take you for a Jesuit carrying orders and we shall have passed the frontiers before they can pursue us."

As he spoke these words he started off at full speed and shouted in Spanish:

"Way, way for the Reverend Father Colonel. . . ."

CHAPTER XVI

What happened to the two travellers with two girls, two monkeys, and the savages called Oreillons

CANDIDE and his valet were past the barriers before anybody in the camp knew of the death of the German Jesuit. The vigilant Cacambo had taken care to fill his saddle-bag with bread, chocolate, ham, fruit, and several bottles of wine. On their Andalusian horses they plunged into an unknown country where they found no road.

At last a beautiful plain traversed by streams met their eyes. Our two travellers put their horses to grass. Cacambo suggested to his master that they should eat and set the example.

"How can you expect me to eat ham," said Candide, " when I have killed the son of My Lord the Baron and find myself condemned never to see the fair Cunegonde again in my life? What is the use of prolonging my miserable days since I must drag them out far from her in remorse and despair? And what will the Journal de Trévoux[1] say?"

Speaking thus, he began to eat. The sun was setting. The two wanderers heard faint cries which seemed to be uttered by women. They could not tell whether these were cries of pain or of joy; but they rose hastily with that alarm and uneasiness caused by everything in an unknown country.

These cries came from two completely naked girls

---

[1] A journal published by the Jesuits.

who were running gently along the edge of the plain, while two monkeys pursued them and bit their buttocks. Candide was moved to pity; he had learned to shoot among the Bulgarians and could have brought down a nut from a tree without touching the leaves. He raised his double-barrelled Spanish gun, fired, and killed the two monkeys.

"God be praised, my dear Cacambo, I have delivered these two poor creatures from a great danger; if I committed a sin by killing an Inquisitor and a Jesuit, I have atoned for it by saving the lives of these two girls. Perhaps they are young ladies of quality and this adventure may be of great advantage to us in this country."

He was going on, but his tongue clove to the roof of his mouth when he saw the two girls tenderly kissing the two monkeys, shedding tears on their bodies and filling the air with the most piteous cries.

"I did not expect so much human kindliness," he said at last to Cacambo, who replied:

"You have performed a wonderful masterpiece; you have killed the two lovers of these young ladies."

"Their lovers! Can it be possible? You are jesting at me, Cacambo; how can I believe you?"

"My dear master," replied Cacambo, "you are always surprised by everything; why should you think it so strange that in some countries there should be monkeys who obtain ladies' favours? They are quarter men, as I am a quarter Spaniard."

"Alas!" replied Candide, "I remember to have heard Dr Pangloss say that similar accidents occurred in the past and that these mixtures produce Aigypans, fauns and satyrs; that several eminent persons of antiquity have seen them; but I thought they were fables."

"You ought now to be convinced that it is true," said Cacambo, "and you see how people behave when they have not received a proper education; the only thing I fear is that these ladies may get us into difficulty."

These wise reflections persuaded Candide to leave the plain and to plunge into the woods. He ate supper there with Cacambo and, after having cursed the Inquisitor of Portugal, the governor of Buenos Ayres and the Baron, they went to sleep on the moss. When they woke up they found they could not move; the reason was that during the night the Oreillons, the inhabitants of the country, to whom they had been denounced by the two ladies, had bound them with ropes made of bark. They were surrounded by fifty naked Oreillons, armed with arrows, clubs and stone hatchets. Some were boiling a large cauldron, others were preparing spits and they were all shouting:

"Here's a Jesuit, here's a Jesuit! We shall be revenged and have a good dinner; let us eat the Jesuit, let us eat the Jesuit!"

"I told you so, my dear master," said Cacambo sadly. "I knew those two girls would play us a dirty trick."

Candide perceived the cauldron and the spits and exclaimed:

"We are certainly going to be roasted or boiled. Ah! What would Dr Pangloss say if he saw what the pure state of nature is? All is well, granted; but I confess it is very cruel to have lost Miss Cunegonde and to be spitted by the Oreillons."

Cacambo never lost his head.

"Do not despair," he said to the wretched Candide. "I understand a little of their dialect and I will speak to them."

"Do not fail," said Candide, "to point out to them the dreadful inhumanity of cooking men and how very unchristian it is."

"Gentlemen," said Cacambo, "you mean to eat a Jesuit to-day? 'Tis a good deed; nothing could be more just than to treat one's enemies in this fashion. Indeed the law of nature teaches us to kill our neighbour and this is how people behave all over the world. If we do not exert the right of eating our neighbour, it is because we have other means of making good cheer; but you have not the same resources as we, and it is certainly better to eat our enemies than to abandon the fruits of victory to ravens and crows. But, gentlemen, you would not wish to eat your friends. You believe you are about to place a Jesuit on the spit, and 'tis your defender, the enemy of your enemies you are about to roast. I was born in your country; the gentleman you see here is my master and, far from being a Jesuit, he has just killed a Jesuit and is wearing his clothes; which is the cause of your mistake. To verify what I say, take his gown, carry it to the first barrier of the kingdom of *Los Padres* and inquire whether my master has not killed a Jesuit officer. It will not take you long and you will have plenty of time to eat us if you find I have lied. But if I have told the truth, you are too well acquainted with the principles of public law, good morals and discipline, not to pardon us."

The Oreillons thought this a very reasonable speech; they deputed two of their notables to go with all diligence and find out the truth. The two deputies acquitted themselves of their task like intelligent men and soon returned with good news.

The Oreillons unbound their two prisoners, overwhelmed them with civilities, offered them girls, gave them refreshment, and accompanied them to the frontiers of their dominions, shouting joyfully:

"He is not a Jesuit, he is not a Jesuit!"

Candide could not cease from wondering at the cause of his deliverance.

"What a nation," said he. "What men! What manners! If I had not been so lucky as to stick my sword through the body of Miss Cunegonde's brother I should infallibly have been eaten. But, after all, there is something good in the pure state of nature, since these people, instead of eating me, offered me a thousand civilities as soon as they knew I was not a Jesuit."

CHAPTER XVII

Arrival of Candide and his valet in the country of Eldorado and what they saw there

WHEN they reached the frontiers of the Oreillons, Cacambo said to Candide:

"You see this hemisphere is no better than the other; take my advice, let us go back to Europe by the shortest road."

"How can we go back," said Candide, "and where can we go? If I go to my own country, the Bulgarians and the Abares are murdering everybody; if I return to Portugal I shall be burned; if we stay here, we run the risk of being spitted at any moment. But how can I make up my mind to leave that part of the world where Miss Cunegonde is living?"

"Let us go to Cayenne," said Cacambo, "we shall find Frenchmen there, for they go all over the world; they might help us. Perhaps God will have pity on us."

It was not easy to go to Cayenne. They knew roughly the direction to take, but mountains, rivers, precipices, brigands and savages were everywhere terrible obstacles. Their horses died of fatigue; their provisions were exhausted; for a whole month they lived on wild fruits and at last found themselves near a little river fringed with coconut-trees which supported their lives and their hopes.

Cacambo, who always gave advice as prudent as the old woman's, said to Candide:

"We can go no farther, we have walked far enough; I can see an empty canoe in the bank, let us fill it with coconuts, get into the little boat and drift with the current; a river always leads to some inhabited place. If we do not find anything pleasant, we shall at least find something new."

"Come on then," said Candide, "and let us trust to Providence."

They drifted for some leagues between banks which were sometimes flowery, sometimes bare, sometimes flat, sometimes steep. The river continually became wider; finally it disappeared under an arch of frightful rocks which towered up to the very sky. The two travellers were bold enough to trust themselves to the current under this arch. The stream, narrowed between walls, carried them with horrible rapidity and noise. After twenty-four hours they saw daylight again; but their canoe was wrecked on reefs; they had to crawl from rock to rock for a whole league and at last they discovered an immense horizon, bordered by inaccessible mountains. The country was cultivated for pleasure as well as for necessity; everywhere the useful was agreeable. The roads were covered or rather ornamented with carriages of brilliant material and shape, carrying men and women of singular beauty, who were rapidly drawn along by large red sheep whose swiftness surpassed that of the finest horses of Andalusia, Tetuan and Mequinez.

"This country," said Candide, "is better than Westphalia."

He landed with Cacambo near the first village he came to. Several children of the village, dressed in torn gold brocade, were playing coits outside the village. Our two men from the other world amused themselves by looking on; their coits were large round pieces, yellow, red and green, which shone with peculiar lustre. The travellers were curious enough to pick up some of them; they were of gold, emeralds and rubies, the least of which would have been the greatest ornament in the Mogul's throne.

"No doubt," said Cacambo, "these children are the sons of the King of this country playing at coits."

At that moment the village schoolmaster appeared to call them into school.

"This," said Candide, "is the tutor of the Royal Family."

The little beggars immediately left their game, abandoning their coits and everything with which they had been playing. Candide picked them up, ran to the tutor, and presented them to him humbly, giving him to understand by signs that their Royal Highnesses had forgotten their gold and their precious stones. The village schoolmaster smiled, threw them on the ground, gazed for a moment at Candide's face with much surprise and continued on his way.

The travellers did not fail to pick up the gold, the rubies and the emeralds.

"Where are we?" cried Candide. "The children of the Kings must be well brought up, since they are taught to despise gold and precious stones."

Cacambo was as much surprised as Candide. At last they reached the first house in the village, which was built like a European palace. There were crowds of people round the door and still more inside; very pleasant music could be heard and there was a delicious smell of cooking. Cacambo went up to the door and heard them speaking Peruvian; it was his maternal tongue, for every one knows that Cacambo was born in a village of Tucuman where nothing else is spoken.

"I will act as your interpreter," he said to Candide, "this is an inn, let us enter."

Immediately two boys and two girls of the inn, dressed in cloth of gold, whose hair was bound up with ribbons, invited them to sit down to the table d'hôte.

They served four soups each garnished with two parrots, a boiled condor which weighed two hundred pounds, two roast monkeys of excellent flavour, three hundred colibris in one dish and six hundred humming-birds in another, exquisite ragouts and delicious pastries, all in dishes of a sort of rock-crystal. The boys and girls brought several sorts of drinks made of sugar-cane. Most of the guests were merchants and coachmen, all extremely polite, who asked Cacambo a few questions with the most delicate discretion and answered his in a satisfactory manner.

When the meal was over, Cacambo, like Candide, thought he could pay the reckoning by throwing on the table two of the large pieces of gold he had picked up; the host and hostess laughed until they had to hold their sides. At last they recovered themselves.

"Gentlemen," said the host, "we perceive you are strangers; we are not accustomed to seeing them. Forgive us if we began to laugh when you offered us in payment the stones from our highways. No doubt you have none of the money of this country, but you do not need any to dine here. All the hotels established for the utility of commerce are paid for by the government. You have been ill-entertained here because this is a poor village; but everywhere else you will be received as you deserve to be."

Cacambo explained to Candide all that the host had said, and Candide listened in the same admiration and disorder with which his friend Cacambo interpreted.

"What can this country be," they said to each other, "which is unknown to the rest of the world and where all nature is so different from ours? Probably it is the country where everything is for the best; for there must be one country of that sort. And, in spite of what Dr Pangloss said, I often noticed that everything went very ill in Westphalia."

64

CHAPTER XVIII

What they saw in the land of Eldorado

CACAMBO informed the host of his curiosity, and the host said:

"I am a very ignorant man and am all the better for it; but we have here an old man who has retired from the court and who is the most learned and most communicative man in the kingdom."

And he at once took Cacambo to the old man. Candide now played only the second part and accompanied his valet.

They entered a very simple house, for the door was only of silver and the panelling of the apartments in gold, but so tastefully carved that the richest decorations did not surpass it. The antechamber indeed was only encrusted with rubies and emeralds; but the order with which everything was arranged atoned for this extreme simplicity.

The old man received the two strangers on a sofa padded with colibri feathers, and presented them with drinks in diamond cups; after which he satisfied their curiosity in these words:

"I am a hundred and seventy-two years old and I heard from my late father, the King's equerry, the astonishing revolutions of Peru of which he had been an eye-witness. The kingdom where we now are is the ancient country of the Incas, who most imprudently left it to conquer part of the world and were at last destroyed by the Spaniards.

"The princes of their family who remained in their native country had more wisdom; with the consent of the nation, they ordered that no inhabitants should ever leave our little kingdom, and this it is that has pre-served our innocence and our felicity. The Spaniards had some vague knowledge of this country, which they called Eldorado, and about a hundred years ago an English-

man named Raleigh came very near to it; but, since we are sur-rounded by inaccessible rocks and precipices, we have hitherto been exempt from the rapacity of the nations of Europe who have an inconceivable lust for the pebbles and mud of our land and would kill us to the last man to get posses-sion of them.''

The conversation was long; it touched upon the form of the government, manners, women, public spectacles and the arts. Finally Candide, who was always interested in metaphysics, asked through Cacambo whether the country had a religion. The old man blushed a little.

"How can you doubt it?" said he. "Do you think we are ingrates?"

Cacambo humbly asked what was the religion of Eldorado. The old man blushed again.

"Can there be two religions?" said he. "We have, I think, the religion of every one else; we adore God from evening until morning."

"Do you adore only one god?" said Cacambo, who continued to act as the interpreter of Candide's doubts.

"Manifestly," said the old man, "there are not two or three or four. I must confess that the people of your world ask very extraordinary questions."

Candide continued to press the old man with questions; he wished to know how they prayed to God in Eldorado.

"We do not pray," said the good and respectable sage, "we have nothing to ask from him; he has given us everything necessary and we continually give him thanks."

Candide was curious to see the priests; and asked where they were. The good old man smiled.

"My friends," said he, "we are all priests; the King and all the heads of families solemnly sing praises every morning, accompanied by five or six thousand musicians."

"What! Have you no monks to teach, to dispute, to govern, to intrigue and to burn people who do not agree with them?"

"For that, we should have to become fools," said the old man; "here we are all of the same opinion and do not understand what you mean with your monks."

At all this Candide was in an ecstasy and said to himself:

"This is very different from Westphalia and the castle of His Lordship the Baron; if our friend Pangloss had seen Eldorado, he would not have said that the castle of Thunder-ten-tronckh was the best of all that exists on the earth; certainly, a man should travel."

After this long conversation the good old man ordered a carriage to be harnessed with six sheep and gave the two travellers twelve of his servants to take them to court.

"You will excuse me," he said, "if my age deprives me of the honour of accompanying you. The King will receive you in a manner which will not displease you and doubtless you will pardon the customs of the country if any of them disconcert you."

Candide and Cacambo entered the carriage; the six sheep galloped off and in less than four hours they reached the King's palace, which was situated at one end of the capital. The portal was two hundred and twenty feet high and a hundred feet wide; it is impossible to describe its material. Anyone can see the prodigious superiority it must have over the pebbles and sand we call *gold* and *gems*.

Twenty beautiful maidens of the guard received Candide and Cacambo as they alighted from the carriage, conducted them to the baths and dressed them in robes woven from the down of colibris; after which the principal male and female officers of the Crown led them to his Majesty's apartment through two files of a thousand musicians each, according to the usual custom. As they approached the throne-room, Cacambo asked one of the chief officers how they should behave in his Majesty's presence; whether they should fall on their knees or flat on their faces, whether they should put their hands on their heads or on their backsides; whether they should lick the dust of the throne-room; in a word, what was the ceremony?

"The custom," said the chief officer, "is to embrace the King and to kiss him on either cheek."

Candide and Cacambo threw their arms round his Majesty's neck; he received them with all imaginable favour and politely asked them to supper.

Meanwhile they were carried to see the town, the public buildings rising to the very skies, the market-places ornamented with thousands of columns, the fountains of pure water, the fountains of rose-water and of liquors distilled from sugar-cane, which played continually in the public squares paved with precious stones which emitted a perfume like that of cloves and cinnamon.

Candide asked to see the law-courts; he was told there were none, and that nobody ever went to law. He asked if there were prisons and was told there were none. He was still more surprised and pleased by the palace of sciences, where he saw a gallery two thousand feet long, filled with instruments of mathematics and physics.

After they had explored all the afternoon about a thousandth part of the town, they were taken back to the King. Candide sat down to table with his Majesty, his valet Cacambo and several ladies. Never was better cheer, and never was anyone wittier at supper than his Majesty. Cacambo explained the King's witty remarks to Candide and even when translated they still appeared witty. Among all the things which amazed Candide, this did not amaze him the least.

They enjoyed this hospitality for a month. Candide repeatedly said to Cacambo:

"Once again, my friend, it is quite true that the castle where I was born cannot be compared with this country; but then Miss Cunegonde is not here and you probably have a mistress in Europe. If we remain here, we shall only be like everyone else; but if we return to our own world with only twelve sheep laden with Eldorado pebbles, we shall be richer than all the kings put together; we shall have no more Inquisitors to fear and we can easily regain Miss Cunegonde."

Cacambo agreed with this; it is so pleasant to be on the move, to show off before friends, to make a parade of the things seen on one's travels, that these two happy men resolved to be so no longer and to ask his Majesty's permission to depart.

"You are doing a very silly thing," said the King. "I know my country is small; but when we are comfortable anywhere we should stay there; I certainly have not the right to detain foreigners, that is a tyranny which does not exist either in our manners or our laws; all men are free, leave when you please, but the way out is very difficult. It is impossible to ascend the rapid river by which you miraculously came here and which flows under arches of rock. The mountains which surround the whole of my kingdom are ten thousand feet high and as perpendicular as rocks; they are more than ten leagues broad and you can only get down from them by way of precipices. However, since you must go, I will give orders to the directors of machinery to make a machine which will carry you comfortably. When you have been taken to the other side of the mountains, nobody can proceed any farther with you; for my subjects have sworn never to pass this boundary and they are too wise to break their oath. Ask anything else of me you wish."

"We ask nothing of your Majesty," said Cacambo, "except a few sheep laden with provisions, pebbles, and the mud of this country."

The King laughed.

"I cannot understand," said he, "the taste you people of Europe have for our yellow mud; but take as much as you wish, and much good may it do you."

He immediately ordered his engineers to make a machine to hoist these two extraordinary men out of his kingdom.

Three thousand learned scientists worked at it; it was ready in a fortnight and only cost about twenty million pounds sterling in the money of that country. Candide and Cacambo were placed on the machine; there were two large red sheep saddled and bridled for them to ride on when they had passed the mountains, twenty sumpter sheep laden with provisions, thirty carrying presents of the most curious productions of the country and fifty laden with gold, precious stones and diamonds. The King embraced the two vagabonds tenderly.

Their departure was a splendid sight and so was the ingenious manner in which they and their sheep were hoisted on to the top of the mountains.

The scientists took leave of them after having landed them safely, and Candide's only desire and object was to go and present Miss Cunegonde with his sheep.

"We have sufficient to pay the governor of Buenos Ayres," said he, "if Miss Cunegonde can be bought. Let us go to Cayenne, and take ship, and then we will see what kingdom we will buy."

CHAPTER XIX

What happened to them at Surinam, and how Candide made the acquaintance of Martin

OUR two travellers' first day was quite pleasant. They were encouraged by the idea of possessing more treasures than all Asia, Europe and Africa could collect. Candide in transport carved the name of Cunegonde on the trees.

On the second day two of the sheep stuck in a marsh and were swallowed up with their loads; two other sheep died of fatigue a few days later; then seven or eight died of hunger in a desert; several days afterwards others fell off precipices. Finally, after they had travelled for a hundred days, they had only two sheep left. Candide said to Cacambo:

"My friend, you see how perishable are the riches of this world; nothing is steadfast but virtue and the happiness of seeing Miss Cunegonde again."

"I admit it," said Cacambo, "but we still have two sheep with more treasures than ever the King of Spain will have, and in the distance I see a town I suspect is Surinam, which belongs to the Dutch. We are at the end of our troubles and the beginning of our happiness."

As they drew near the town they met a negro lying on the ground wearing only half his clothes, that is to say, a pair of blue cotton drawers; this poor man had no left leg and no right hand.

"Good Heavens!" said Candide to him in Dutch, "what are you doing there, my friend, in this horrible state?"

"I am waiting for my master, the famous merchant Mr Vanderdendur."

"Was it Mr Vanderdendur," said Candide, "who treated you in this way?"

"Yes, sir," said the negro, "it is the custom. We are given a pair of cotton drawers twice a year as clothing. When we work in the sugar-mills and the grindstone catches our fingers, they cut off the hand; when we try to run away, they cut off a leg. Both these things happened to me. This is the price paid for the sugar you eat in Europe. But when my mother sold me for ten patagons on the coast of Guinea, she said to me: My dear child, give thanks to our fetishes, always worship them, and they will make you happy; you have the honour to be a slave of our lords the white men and thereby you have made the fortune of your father and mother.' Alas! I do not know whether I made their fortune, but they certainly did not make mine. Dogs, monkeys and parrots are a thousand times less miserable then we are; the Dutch fetishes who converted me tell me every Sunday that we are all of us, whites and blacks, the children of Adam. I am not a genealogist, but if these preachers tell the truth, we are all second cousins. Now, you will admit that no one could treat his relatives in a more horrible way."

"O Pangloss!" cried Candide. "This is an abomination you had not guessed; this is too much, in the end I shall have to renounce optimism."

"What is optimism?" said Cacambo.

"Alas!" said Candide, "it is the mania of maintaining that everything is well when we are wretched."

And he shed tears as he looked at his negro; and he entered Surinam weeping.

The first thing they inquired was whether there was any ship in the port which could be sent to Buenos Ayres. The person they addressed happened to be a

73

Spanish captain, who offered to strike an honest bargain with them. He arranged to meet them at an inn. Candide and the faithful Cacambo went and waited for him with their two sheep.

Candide, who blurted everything out, told the Spaniard all his adventures and confessed that he wanted to elope with Miss Cunegonde.

"I shall certainly not take you to Buenos Ayres," said the captain. "I should be hanged and you would too. The fair Cunegonde is his Lordship's favourite mistress."

Candide was thunderstruck; he sobbed for a long time; then he took Cacambo aside.

"My dear friend," said he, "this is what you must do. We each have in our pockets five or six million pound's worth of diamonds; you are more skilful than I am; go to Buenos Ayres and get Miss Cunegonde. If the governor makes any difficulties give him a million; if he is still obstinate give him two; you have not killed an Inquisitor, so they will not suspect you. I will fit out another ship, I will go and wait for you at Venice; it is a free country where there is nothing to fear from Bulgarians, Abares, Jews or Inquisitors."

Cacambo applauded this wise resolution; he was in despair at leaving a good master who had become his intimate friend; but the pleasure of being useful to him overcame the grief of leaving him. They embraced with tears. Candide urged him not to forget the good old woman. Cacambo set off that very same day; he was a very good man, this Cacambo.

Candide remained some time longer at Surinam waiting for another captain to take him to Italy with the two sheep he had left. He engaged servants and bought everything necessary for a long voyage. At last Mr Vanderdendur, the owner of a large ship, came to see him.

"How much do you want," he asked this man, "to take me straight to Venice with my servants, my baggage and these two sheep?"

The captain asked for ten thousand piastres. Candide did not hesitate.

"Oh! Ho!" said the prudent Vanderdendur to himself, "this foreigner gives ten thousand piastres immediately! He must be very rich."

He returned a moment afterwards and said he could not sail for less than twenty thousand.

"Very well, you shall have them," said Candide.

"Whew!" said the merchant to himself, "this man gives twenty thousand piastres as easily as ten thousand."

He came back again, and said he could not take him to Venice for less than thirty thousand piastres.

"Then you shall have thirty thousand," replied Candide.

"Oho!" said the Dutch merchant to himself again, "thirty thousand piastres is nothing to this man; obviously the two sheep are laden with immense treasures; I will not insist any further; first let me make him pay the thirty thousand piastres, and then we will see."

Candide sold two little diamonds, the smaller of which was worth more than all the money the captain asked. He paid him in advance. The two sheep were taken on board. Candide followed in a little boat to join the ship which rode at anchor; the captain watched his time, set his sails and weighed anchor; the wind was favourable. Candide, bewildered and stupefied, soon lost sight of him.

"Alas!" he cried, "this is a trick worthy of the old world."

He returned to shore, in grief; for he had lost enough to make the fortune of twenty kings.

He went to the Dutch judge; and, as he was rather

disturbed, he knocked loudly at the door; he went in, related what had happened and talked a little louder than he ought to have done. The judge began by fining him ten thousand piastres for the noise he had made; he then listened patiently to him, promised to look into his affair as soon as the merchant returned, and charged him another ten thousand piastres for the expenses of the audience.

This behaviour reduced Candide to despair; he had indeed endured misfortunes a thousand times more painful; but the calmness of the judge and of the captain who had robbed him, stirred up his bile and plunged him into a black melancholy. The malevolence of men revealed itself to his mind in all its ugliness; he entertained only gloomy ideas. At last a French ship was about to leave for Bordeaux and, since he no longer had any sheep laden with diamonds to put on board, he hired a cabin at a reasonable price and announced throughout the town that he would give the passage, food and two thousand piastres to an honest man who would make the journey with him, on condition that this man was the most unfortunate and the most disgusted with his condition in the whole province.

Such a crowd of applicants arrived that a fleet would not have contained them. Candide, wishing to choose among the most likely, picked out twenty persons who seemed reasonably sociable and who all claimed to deserve his preference. He collected them in a tavern and gave them supper, on condition that each took an oath to relate truthfully the story of his life, promising that he would choose the man who seemed to him the most deserving of pity and to have the most cause for being discontented with his condition, and that he would give the others a little money.

The sitting lasted until four o'clock in the morning. As Candide listened to their adventures he remembered what the old woman had said on the voyage to Buenos Ayres and how she had wagered that there was nobody on the boat who had not experienced very great misfortunes. At each story which was told him, he thought of Pangloss.

"This Pangloss," said he, "would have some difficulty in supporting his system. I wish he were here. Certainly, if everything is well, it is only in Eldorado and not in the rest of the world."

He finally determined in favour of a poor man of letters who had worked ten years for the booksellers at Amsterdam. He judged that there was no occupation in the world which could more disgust a man.

This man of letters, who was also a good man, had been robbed by his wife, beaten by his son, and abandoned by his daughter, who had eloped with a Portuguese. He had just been deprived of a small post on which he depended and the preachers of Surinam were persecuting him because they thought he was a Socinian.

It must be admitted that the others were at least as unfortunate as he was; but Candide hoped that this learned man would help to pass the time during the voyage. All his other rivals considered that Candide was doing them a great injustice; but he soothed them down by giving each of them a hundred piastres.

CHAPTER XX

What happened to Candide and Martin at sea

So the old man, who was called Martin, embarked with Candide for Bordeaux. Both had seen and suffered much; and if the ship had been sailing from Surinam to Japan by way of the Cape of Good Hope they would have been able to discuss moral and physical evil during the whole voyage.

However, Candide had one great advantage over Martin, because he still hoped to see Miss Cunegonde again, and Martin had nothing to hope for; moreover, he possessed gold and diamonds; and, although he had lost a hundred large red sheep laden with the greatest treasures on earth, although he was still enraged at being robbed by the Dutch captain, yet when he thought of what he still had left in his pockets and when he talked of Cunegonde, especially at the end of a meal, he still inclined towards the system of Pangloss.

"But what do you think of all this, Mr Martin?" said he to the man of letters. "What is your view of moral and physical evil?"

"Sir," replied Martin, "my priests accused me of being a Socinian; but the truth is I am a Manichæan."

"You are poking fun at me," said Candide, "there are no Manichæans left in the world."

"I am one," said Martin. "I don't know what to do about it, but I am unable to think in any other fashion."

"You must be possessed by the devil," said Candide.

"He takes so great a share in the affairs of this world," said Martin, "that he might well be in me, as

79

he is everywhere else; but I confess that when I consider this globe, or rather this globule, I think that God has abandoned it to some evil creature—always excepting Eldorado. I have never seen a town which did not desire the ruin of the next town, never a family which did not wish to exterminate some other family. Everywhere the weak loathe the powerful before whom they cower and the powerful treat them like flocks of sheep whose wool and flesh are to be sold. A million drilled assassins go from one end of Europe to the other murdering and robbing with discipline in order to earn their bread, because there is no honester occupation; and in the towns which seem to enjoy peace and where the arts flourish, men are devoured by more envy, troubles and worries than the afflictions of a besieged town. Secret griefs are even more cruel than public miseries. In a word, I have seen so much and endured so much that I have become a Manichæan."

"Yet there is some good," replied Candide.

"There may be," said Martin, "but I do not know it."

In the midst of this dispute they heard the sound of cannon. The noise increased every moment. Every one took his telescope. About three miles away they saw two ships engaged in battle; and the wind brought them so near the French ship that they had the pleasure of seeing the fight at their ease. At last one of the two ships fired a broadside so accurately and so low down that the other ship began to sink. Candide and Martin distinctly saw a hundred men on the main deck of the sinking ship; they raised their hands to Heaven and uttered frightful shrieks; in a moment all was engulfed.

"Well!" said Martin, "that is how men treat each other."

"It is certainly true," said Candide, "that there is something diabolical in this affair."

As he was speaking, he saw something of a brilliant red swimming near the ship. They launched a boat to see what it could be; it was one of his sheep. Candide felt more joy at recovering this sheep than grief at losing a hundred all laden with large diamonds from Eldorado.

The French captain soon perceived that the captain of the remaining ship was a Spaniard and that the sunken ship was a Dutch pirate; the captain was the very same who had robbed Candide. The immense wealth this scoundrel had stolen was swallowed up with him in the sea and only a sheep was saved.

"You see," said Candide to Martin, "that crime is sometimes punished; this scoundrel of a Dutch captain has met the fate he deserved."

"Yes," said Martin, "but was it necessary that the other passengers on his ship should perish too? God punished the thief, and the devil drowned the others."

Meanwhile the French and Spanish ships continued on their way and Candide continued his conversation with Martin. They argued for a fortnight and at the end of the fortnight they had got no further than at the beginning. But after all, they talked, they exchanged ideas, they consoled each other. Candide stroked his sheep.

"Since I have found you again," said he, "I may very likely find Cunegonde."

CHAPTER XXI

Candide and Martin approach the coast of France and argue

AT last they sighted the coast of France.

"Have you ever been to France, Mr. Martin?" said Candide.

"Yes," said Martin, "I have traversed several provinces. In some half the inhabitants are crazy, in others they are too artful, in some they are usually quite gentle and stupid, and in others they think they are clever; in all of them the chief occupation is making love, the second scandal-mongering and the third talking nonsense."

"But, Mr Martin, have you seen Paris?"

"Yes, I have seen Paris; it is a mixture of all these species; it is a chaos, a throng where everybody hunts for pleasure and hardly anybody finds it, at least so far as I could see. I did not stay there long; when I arrived there I was robbed of everything I had by pickpockets at Saint-Germain's fair; they thought I was a thief and I spent a week in prison; after which I became a printer's reader to earn enough to return to Holland on foot. I met the scribbling rabble, the intriguing rabble and the fanatical rabble. We hear that there are very polite people in the town; I am glad to think so."

"For my part, I have not the least curiosity to see France," said Candide. "You can easily guess that when a man has spent a month in Eldorado he cares to see nothing else in the world but Miss Cunegonde. I shall go and wait for her at Venice; we will go to Italy by way of France; will you come with me?"

"Willingly," said Martin. "They say that Venice is

only good for the Venetian nobles, but that foreigners are nevertheless well received when they have plenty of money; I have none, you have plenty, I will follow you anywhere."

"Apropos," said Candide, "do you think the earth was originally a sea, as we are assured by that large book[1] belonging to the captain?"

"I don't believe it in the least," said Martin, "any more than all the other whimsies we have been pestered with recently!"

"But to what end was this world formed?" said Candide.

"To infuriate us," replied Martin.

"Are you not very much surprised," continued Candide, "by the love those two girls of the country of the Oreillons had for those two monkeys, whose adventure I told you?"

"Not in the least," said Martin. "I see nothing strange in their passion; I have seen so many extraordinary things that nothing seems extraordinary to me."

"Do you think," said Candide, "that men have always massacred each other, as they do to-day? Have they always been liars, cheats, traitors, brigands, weak, flighty, cowardly, envious, gluttonous, drunken, grasping, and vicious, bloody, backbiting, debauched, fanatical, hypocritical and silly?"

"Do you think," said Martin, "that sparrow-hawks have always eaten the pigeons they came across?"

"Yes, of course," said Candide.

"Well," said Martin, "if sparrow-hawks have always possessed the same nature, why should you expect men to change theirs?"

"Oh!" said Candide, "there is a great difference; free-will. . . ."

Arguing thus, they arrived at Bordeaux.

[1] The Bible.

83

CHAPTER XXII

What happened to Candide and Martin in France

CANDIDE remained in Bordeaux only long enough to sell a few Eldorado pebbles and to provide himself with a two-seated post-chaise, for he could no longer get on without his philosopher Martin; but he was very grieved at having to part with his sheep, which he left with the Academy of Sciences at Bordeaux. The Academy offered as the subject for a prize that year the cause of the redness of the sheep's fleece; and the prize was awarded to a learned man in the North, who proved by A plus B minus C divided by Z that the sheep must be red and die of the sheep-pox.

However all the travellers Candide met in taverns on the way said to him: "We are going to Paris." This general eagerness at length made him wish to see that capital; it was not far out of the road to Venice.

He entered by the Faubourg Saint-Marceau and thought he was in the ugliest village of Westphalia.

Candide had scarcely reached his inn when he was attacked by a slight illness caused by fatigue. As he wore an enormous diamond on his finger, and a prodigiously heavy strong-box had been observed in his train, he immediately had with him two doctors he had not asked for, several intimate friends who would not leave him and two devotees who kept making him broth. Said Martin:

"I remember that I was ill too when I first came to Paris; I was very poor; so I had no friends, no devotees, no doctors, and I got well."

However, with the aid of medicine and bloodletting,

84

Candide's illness became serious. An inhabitant of the district came and gently asked him for a note payable to bearer in the next world; Candide would have nothing to do with it. The devotees assured him that it was a new fashion;[1] Candide replied that he was not a fashionable man. Martin wanted to throw the inhabitant out of the window; the clerk swore that Candide should not be buried; Martin swore that he would bury the clerk if he continued to annoy them. The quarrel became heated; Martin took him by the shoulders and turned him out roughly; this caused a great scandal, and they made an official report on it.

Candide got better; and during his convalescence he had very good company to supper with him. They gambled for high stakes. Candide was vastly surprised that he never drew an ace; and Martin was not surprised at all.

Among those who did the honours of the town was a little abbé from Périgord, one of those assiduous people who are always alert, always obliging, impudent, fawning, accommodating, always on the look-out for the arrival of foreigners, ready to tell them all the scandals of the town and to procure them pleasures at any price. This abbé took Candide and Martin to the theatre. A new tragedy was being played. Candide was seated near several wits. This did not prevent his weeping at perfectly played scenes. One of the argumentative bores near him said during an interval:

"You have no business to weep, this is a very bad actress, the actor playing with her is still worse, the play is still worse than the actors; the author does not know a word of Arabic and yet the scene is in Arabia; moreover, he is a man who does not believe in innate ideas; to-morrow I will bring you twenty articles written against him."

---

[1] A ticket of confession.

"Sir," said Candide to the abbé, "how many plays have you in France?"

"Five or six thousand," he replied.

"That's a lot," said Candide, "and how many good ones are there?"

"Fifteen or sixteen," replied the other.

"That's a lot," said Martin.

Candide was greatly pleased with an actress who took the part of Queen Elizabeth in a rather dull tragedy which is sometimes played.

"This actress," said he to Martin, "pleases me very much; she looks rather like Miss Cunegonde; I should be very glad to pay her my respects."

The abbé offered to introduce him to her. Candide, brought up in Germany, asked what was the etiquette, and how queens of England were treated in France.

"There is a distinction," said the abbé. "In the provinces we take them to a tavern; in Paris we respect them when they are beautiful and throw them in the public sewer when they are dead."

"Queens in the public sewer!" said Candide.

"Yes, indeed," said Martin, "the abbé is right; I was in Paris when Miss Monime[1] departed, as they say, this life; she was refused what people here call the *honours of burial*—that is to say, the honour of rotting with all the beggars of the district in a horrible cemetery; she was buried by herself at the corner of the Rue de Bourgogne; which must have given her extreme pain, for her mind was very lofty."

"That was very impolite," said Candide.

"What do you expect?" said Martin. "These people are like that. Imagine all possible contradictions and incompatibilities; you will see them in the government, in the law-courts, in the churches and the entertainments of this absurd nation."

---

[1] Adrienne Lecouvreur.

"It is true that people are always laughing in Paris?" said Candide.

"Yes," said the abbé, "but it is with rage in their hearts, for they complain of everything with roars of laughter, and they even commit with laughter the most detestable actions."

"Who is that fat pig," said Candide, "who said so much ill of the play I cried at so much and of the actors who gave me so much pleasure?"

"He is a living evil," replied the abbé, "who earns his living by abusing all plays and all books; he hates anyone who succeeds, as eunuchs hate those who enjoy; he is one of the serpents of literature who feed on filth and venom; he is a scribbler."

"What do you mean by a scribbler?" said Candide.

"A scribbler of periodical sheets," said the abbé. "A Fréron."

Candide, Martin and the abbé from Périgord talked in this manner on the stairway as they watched everybody going out after the play.

"Although I am most anxious to see Miss Cunegonde again," said Candide, "I should like to sup with Miss Clairon, for I thought her admirable."

The abbé was not the sort of man to know Miss Clairon, for she saw only good company.

"She is engaged this evening," he said, "but I shall have the honour to take you to the house of a lady of quality, and there you will learn as much of Paris as if you had been here for four years."

Candide, who was naturally curious, allowed himself to be taken to the lady's house at the far end of the Faubourg Saint-Honoré; they were playing faro; twelve gloomy punters each held a small hand of cards, the foolish register of their misfortunes. The silence was profound, the punters were pale, the banker was uneasy, and the lady of the house, seated beside this pitiless banker, watched with lynx's eyes every double stake, every seven-and-the-go, with which each player marked his cards; she had them un-marked with severe but polite attention, for fear of losing her customers; the lady called herself Marquise de Parolignac. Her fifteen-year-old daughter was among the punters and winked at her to let her know the tricks of the poor people who attempted to repair the cruelties of fate. The abbé from Périgord, Candide and Martin entered; nobody rose, nobody greeted them, nobody looked at them; every one was profoundly occupied with the cards.

"Her Ladyship the Baroness of Thunder-ten-tronckh was more civil," said Candide.

However the abbé whispered in the ear of the Marquise, who half rose, honoured Candide with a gracious smile and Martin with a most noble nod. Candide was given a seat and a hand of cards, and lost fifty thousand francs in two hands; after which they supped very merrily and every one was surprised that Candide was not more disturbed by his loss. The lackeys said to each other, in the language of lackeys:

"He must be an English Milord."

The supper was like most suppers in Paris; first there was a silence and then a noise of indistinguishable words, then jokes, most of which were insipid, false news, false arguments, some politics and a great deal of scandal; there was even some talk of new books.

"Have you seen," said the abbé from Périgord, "the novel by Gauchat, the doctor of theology?"

"Yes," replied one of the guests, "but I could not finish it. We have a crowd of silly writings, but all of them together do not approach the silliness of Gauchat, doctor of theology. I am so weary of this immensity of detestable books which inundates us that I have taken to faro."

"And what do you say about the *Melanges* by Arch-deacon T.?" said the abbé.

"Ah!" said Madame de Parolignac, "the tiresome creature! How carefully he tells you what everybody knows! How heavily he discusses what is not worth the trouble of being lightly mentioned! How witlessly he appropriates other people's wit! How he spoils what he steals! How he disgusts me! But he will not disgust me any more; it is enough to have read a few pages by the Archdeacon."

There was a man of learning and taste at table who confirmed what the marchioness had said. They then talked of tragedies; the lady asked why there were tragedies which were sometimes played and yet were unreadable. The man of taste explained very clearly how a play might have some interest and hardly any merit; in a few words he proved that it was not suffi-cient to bring in one or two of the situations which are found in all novels and which always attract the spectators; but that a writer of tragedies must be original without being bizarre, often sublime and always natural, must know the human heart and be able to give it speech, must be a great poet but not let any character in his play appear to be a poet, must know his language perfectly, speak it with purity, with continual harmony and never allow the sense to be spoilt for the sake of the rhyme.

"Anyone," he added, "who does not observe all these rules may produce one or two tragedies ap-plauded in the theatre, but he will never be ranked among good writers; there are very few good tragedies; some are idylls in well-written and well-rhymed dia-logue; some are political arguments which send one to sleep, or repulsive amplifications; others are the dreams of an enthusiast, in a barbarous style, with broken dialogue, long apostrophes to the gods (because he does

89

not know how to speak to men), false maxims and turgid commonplaces."

Candide listened attentively to these remarks and conceived a great idea of the speaker; and, as the marchioness had been careful to place him beside her, he leaned over to her ear and took the liberty of asking her who was the man who talked so well.

"He is a man of letters," said the lady, "who does not play cards and is sometimes brought here to supper by the abbé; he has a perfect knowledge of tragedies and books, and he has written a tragedy which was hissed and a book of which only one copy has ever been seen outside his bookseller's shop, and that was one he gave me."

"The great man!" said Candide. "He is another Pangloss."

Then, turning to him, Candide said:

"Sir, no doubt you think that all is for the best in the physical world and in the moral, and that nothing could be otherwise than as it is?"

"Sir," replied the man of letters, "I do not think anything of the sort. I think everything goes awry with us, that nobody knows his rank or his office, nor what he is doing, nor what he ought to do, and that except at supper, which is quite gay and where there appears to be a certain amount of sociability, all the rest of their time is passed in senseless quarrels: Jansenists with Molinists, lawyers with churchmen, men of letters with men of letters, courtiers with courtiers, financiers with the people, wives with husbands, relatives with relatives—'tis an eternal war."

Candide replied:

"I have seen worse things; but a wise man, who has since had the misfortune to be hanged, taught me that it is all for the best; these are only the shadows in a fair picture."

"Your wise man who was hanged was poking fun at the world," said Martin; "and your shadows are horrible stains."

"The stains are made by men," said Candide, "and they cannot avoid them."

"Then it is not their fault," said Martin.

Most of the gamblers, who had not the slightest understanding of this kind of talk, were drinking;

Martin argued with the man of letters and Candide told the hostess some of his adventures.

After supper the marchioness took Candide into a side room and made him sit down on a sofa.

"Well!" said she, "so you are still madly in love with Miss Cunegonde of Thunder-ten-tronckh?"

"Yes, madam," replied Candide.

The marchioness replied with a tender smile:

"You answer like a man from Westphalia. A Frenchman would have said: 'It is true that I was in love with Miss Cunegonde, but when I see you, madam, I fear lest I should cease to love her.' ' '

"Alas! madam," said Candide, "I will answer as you wish."

"Your passion for her," said the marchioness, "began by picking up her handkerchief; I want you to pick up my garter."

"With all my heart," said Candide; and he picked it up.

"But I want you to put it on again," said the lady; and Candide put it on again.

"You see," said the lady, "you are a foreigner; I sometimes make my lovers in Paris languish for a fortnight, but I give myself to you the very first night, because one must do the honours of one's country to a young man from Westphalia."

The fair lady, having perceived two enormous diamonds on the young foreigner's hands, praised them so sincerely that they passed from Candide's fingers to the fingers of the marchioness.

As Candide went home with his abbé from Périgord, he felt some remorse at having been unfaithful to Miss Cunegonde. The abbé sympathised with his distress; he had only had a small share in the fifty thousand francs Candide had lost at cards and in the value of the two half-given, half-extorted, diamonds. His plan was to profit as much as he could from the advantages which his acquaintance with Candide might procure for him. He talked a lot about Cunegonde and Candide told him that he should ask that fair one's forgiveness for his infidelity when he saw her at Venice.

The abbé from Périgord redoubled his politeness and civilities and took a tender interest in all Candide said, in all he did, and in all he wished to do.

"Then, sir," said he, "you are to meet her at Venice?"

"Yes, sir," said Candide, "without fail I must go

and meet Miss Cunegonde there."

Then, carried away by the pleasure of talking about the person he loved, he related, as he was accustomed to do, some of his adventures with that illustrious Westphalian lady.

"I suppose," said the abbé, "that Miss Cunegonde has a great deal of wit and that she writes charming letters."

"I have never received any from her," said Candide, "for you must know that when I was expelled from the castle because of my love for her, I could not write to her; soon afterwards I heard she was dead, then I found her again and then I lost her, and now I have sent an express messenger to her two thousand five hundred leagues from here and am expecting her reply.'

The abbé listened attentively and seemed rather meditative. He soon took leave of the two foreigners after having embraced them tenderly. The next morning when Candide woke up he received a letter composed as follows:

"SIR, my dearest lover, I have been ill for a week in this town; I have just heard that you are here. I should fly to your arms if I could stir. I heard that you had passed through Bordeaux; I left the faithful Cacambo and the old woman there and they will soon follow me. The governor of Buenos Ayres took everything, but I still have your heart. Come, your presence will restore me to life or will make me die of pleasure."

This charming, this unhoped-for letter, transported Candide with inexpressible joy; and the illness of his dear Cunegonde overwhelmed him with grief. Torn between these two sentiments, he took his gold and his diamonds and drove with Martin to the hotel where Miss Cunegonde was staying. He entered trembling with emotion, his heart beat, his voice was broken; he wanted to open the bed-curtains and to have a light brought.

"Do nothing of the sort," said the waiting-maid. "Light would be the death of her."

And she quickly drew the curtains.

"My dear Cunegonde," said Candide, weeping, "how do you feel? If you cannot see me, at least speak to me."

"She cannot speak," said the maid-servant.

The lady then extended a plump hand, which Candide watered with his tears and then filled with diamonds, leaving a bag full of gold in the arm-chair.

In the midst of these transports a police-officer arrived, followed by the abbé from Périgord and a squad of policemen.

"So these are the two suspicious foreigners?" he said.

He had them arrested immediately and ordered his bravoes to hale them off to prison.

"This is not the way they treat travellers in Eldorado," said Candide.

"I am more of a Manichæan than ever," said Martin.

"But, sir, where are you taking us?" said Candide.

"To the deepest dungeon," said the police-officer.

Martin, having recovered his coolness, decided that the lady who pretended to be Cunegonde was a cheat, that the abbé from Périgord was a cheat who had abused Candide's innocence with all possible speed, and that the police-officer was another cheat of whom they could easily be rid.

Rather than expose himself to judicial proceedings, Candide, enlightened by this advice and impatient to see the real Cunegonde again, offered the police-officer three little diamonds worth about three thousand pounds each.

"Ah! sir," said the man with the ivory stick, "if you had committed all imaginable crimes you would be the most honest man in the world. Three diamonds! Worth three thousand pounds each! Sir! I would be killed for your sake, instead of taking you to prison. All strangers are arrested here, but trust to me. I have a brother at Dieppe in Normandy, I will take you there; and if you have any diamonds to give him he will take as much care of you as myself."

"And why are all strangers arrested?" said Candide.

The abbé from Périgord then spoke and said:

"It is because a scoundrel from Atrebatum[1] listened to imbecilities; this alone made him commit a parricide, not like that of May 1610,[2] but like that of December 1594,[3] and like several others committed in other years and in other months by other scoundrels who had listened to imbecilities."

The police-officer then explained what it was all about.

"Ah! the monsters!" cried Candide. "What! Can such horrors be in a nation which dances and sings! Can I not leave at once this country where monkeys torment tigers? I have seen bears in my own country; Eldorado is the only place where I have seen men. In God's name, sir, take me to Venice, where I am to wait for Miss Cunegonde."

"I can only take you to Lower Normandy," said the barigel.[4]

Immediately he took off his irons, said there had been a mistake, sent his men away, took Candide and Martin to Dieppe, and left them with his brother. There was a small Dutch vessel in the port. With the help of three other diamonds the Norman became the most obliging of men and embarked Candide and his

---

[1] Artois. Damiens, who attempted the life of Louis XV on the 5th January 1757 was born at Arras.
[2] Henri IV was assassinated on the 14th May 1610.
[3] On the 27th December 1594, Jean Chatel made an attempt on the life of Henri IV.
[4] Captain of Italian archers or sbirri.

servants in the ship which was about to sail for Portsmouth in England. It was not the road to Venice; but Candide felt as if he had escaped from Hell, and he had every intention of taking the road to Venice at the first opportunity.

CHAPTER XXIII

Candide and Martin reach the coast of England; and what they saw there

"AH! Pangloss, Pangloss! Ah! Martin, Martin! Ah! my dear Cunegonde! What sort of a world is this?" said Cunegonde on the Dutch ship.

"Something very mad and very abominable," replied Martin.

"You know England; are the people there as mad as they are in France?"

" 'Tis another sort of madness," said Martin. "You know these two nations are at war for a few acres of snow in Canada, and that they are spending more on this fine war than all Canada is worth. It is beyond my poor capacity to tell you whether there are more mad-men in one country than in the other; all I know is that in general the people we are going to visit are extremely melancholic."

Talking thus, they arrived at Portsmouth. There were multitudes of people on the shore, looking attentively at a rather fat man who was kneeling down with his eyes bandaged on the deck of one of the ships in the fleet; four soldiers placed opposite this man each shot three bullets into his brain in the calmest manner imaginable; and the whole assembly returned home with great satisfaction.

"What is all this?" said Candide. "And what Demon exercises his power everywhere?"

He asked who was the fat man who had just been killed so ceremoniously.

"An admiral,"[1] was the reply.

"And why kill the admiral?"

"Because," he was told, "he did not kill enough people. He fought a battle with a French admiral and it was held that the English admiral was not close enough to him."

"But," said Candide, "the French admiral was just as far from the English admiral as he was from the French admiral!"

"That is indisputable," was the answer, "but in this country it is a good thing to kill an admiral from time to time to encourage the others."

Candide was so bewildered and so shocked by what he saw and heard that he would not even set foot on shore, but bargained with the Dutch captain (even if he had to pay him as much as the Surinam robber) to take him at once to Venice.

The captain was ready in two days. They sailed down the coast of France; and passed in sight of Lisbon, at which Candide shuddered. They entered the Straits and the Mediterranean and at last reached Venice.

"Praised be God!" said Candide, embracing Martin, "here I shall see the fair Cunegonde again. I trust Cacambo as I would myself. All is well, all goes well, all goes as well as it possibly could."

---

[1] Admiral Byng, shot on the 14th March, 1757, after his defeat near Minorca. Voltaire did all he could to save Byng's life.

CHAPTER XXIV

Paquette and Friar Giroflée

As soon as he reached Venice, he inquired for Cacambo in all the taverns, in all the cafés, and of all the ladies of pleasure; and did not find him. Every day he sent out messengers to all ships and boats; but there was no news of Cacambo.

"What!" said he to Martin, "I have had time to sail from Surinam to Bordeaux, to go from Bordeaux to Paris, from Paris to Dieppe, from Dieppe to Portsmouth, to sail along the coasts of Portugal and Spain, to cross the Mediterranean, to spend several months at Venice, and the fair Cunegonde has not yet arrived! Instead of her I have met only a jade and an abbé from Périgord! Cunegonde is certainly dead and the only thing left for me is to die too. Ah! It would have been better to stay in the Paradise of Eldorado instead of returning to this accursed Europe. How right you are, my dear Martin! Everything is illusion and calamity!"

He fell into a black melancholy and took no part in the opera à la mode or in the other carnival amusements; not a lady caused him the least temptation. Martin said:

"You are indeed simple-minded to suppose that a half-breed valet with five or six millions in his pocket will go and look for your mistress at the other end of the world and bring her to you at Venice. If he finds her, he will take another. I advise you to forget your valet Cacambo and your mistress Cunegonde."

Martin was not consoling. Candide's melancholy increased, and Martin persisted in proving to him that

99

there was little virtue and small happiness in the world
except perhaps in Eldorado where nobody could go.

While arguing about this important subject and
waiting for Cunegonde, Candide noticed a young

Theatine in the Piazza San Marco, with a girl on his arm. The Theatine looked fresh, plump and vigorous; his eyes were bright, his air assured, his countenance firm, and his step lofty. The girl was very pretty and was singing; she gazed amorously at her Theatine and every now and then pinched his fat cheeks.

"At least you will admit," said Candide to Martin, "that those people are happy. Hitherto I have only found unfortunates in the whole habitable earth, except in Eldorado; but I wager that this girl and the Theatine are very happy creatures."

"I wager they are not," said Martin.

"We have only to ask them to dinner," said Candide, "and you will see whether I am wrong."

He immediately accosted them, paid his respects to them, and invited them to come to his hotel to eat macaroni, Lombardy partridges, and caviare, and to drink Montepulciano, Lacryma Christi, Cyprus and Samos wine. The young lady blushed, the Theatine accepted the invitation, and the girl followed, looking at Candide with surprise and confusion in her eyes which were filled with a few tears. Scarcely had they entered Candide's room when she said:

"What! Mr Candide does not recognise Paquette!"

At these words Candide, who had not looked at her very closely because he was occupied entirely by Cunegonde, said to her:

"Alas! my poor child, so it was you who put Dr Pangloss into the fine state I saw him in?"

"Alas! sir, it was indeed," said Paquette. "I see you have heard all about it. I have heard of the terrible misfortunes which happened to Her Ladyship the Baroness's whole family and to the fair Cunegonde. I swear to you that my fate has been just as sad. I was very innocent when you knew me. A Franciscan friar who was my confessor easily seduced me. The results were

101

dreadful; I was obliged to leave the castle shortly after His Lordship the Baron expelled you by kicking you hard and frequently in the backside. If a famous doctor had not taken pity on me I should have died. For some time I was the doctor's mistress from gratitude to him. His wife, who was madly jealous, beat me every day relentlessly; she was a fury. The doctor was the ugliest of men, and I was the most unhappy of all living creatures at being continually beaten on account of a man I did not love. You know, sir, how dangerous it is for a shrewish woman to be the wife of a doctor. One day, exasperated by his wife's behaviour, he gave her some medicine for a little cold, and it was so efficacious that she died two hours afterwards in horrible convulsions. The lady's relatives brought a criminal prosecution against the husband; he fled and I was put in prison. My innocence would not have saved me if I had not been rather pretty. The judge set me free on condition that he took the doctor's place. I was soon supplanted by a rival, expelled without a penny, and obliged to continue the abominable occupation which to you men seems so amusing and which to us is nothing but an abyss of misery. I came to Venice to practise this profession. Ah! sir, if you could imagine what it is to be forced to caress impartially an old tradesman, a lawyer, a monk, a gondolier, an abbé; to be exposed to every insult and outrage; to be reduced often to borrow a petticoat in order to go and find some disgusting man who will lift it; to be robbed by one of what one has earned with another, to be despoiled by the police, and to contemplate for the future nothing but a dreadful old age, a hospital and a dunghill, you would conclude that I am one of the most unfortunate creatures in the world."

Paquette opened her heart in this way to Candide in a side room, in the presence of Martin, who said to Candide:

"You see, I have already won half my wager."

Friar Giroflée had remained in the dining-room, drinking a glass while he waited for dinner.

"But," said Candide to Paquette, "when I met you, you looked so gay, so happy; you were singing, you were caressing the Theatine so naturally; you seemed to me to be as happy as you say you are unfortunate."

"Ah! sir," replied Paquette, "that is one more misery of our profession. Yesterday I was robbed and beaten by an officer, and to-day I must seem to be in a good humour to please a monk."

Candide wanted to hear no more; he admitted that Martin was right. They sat down to table with Paquette and the Theatine. The meal was quite amusing and towards the end they were talking with some confidence.

"Father," said Candide to the monk, "you seem to me to enjoy a fate which everybody should envy; the flower of health shines on your cheek, your face is radiant with happiness; you have a very pretty girl for your recreation and you appear to be very well pleased with your state of life as a Theatine."

"Faith, sir," said Friar Giroflée, "I wish all the Theatines were at the bottom of the sea. A hundred times I have been tempted to set fire to the monastery and to go and be a Turk. My parents forced me at the age of fifteen to put on this detestable robe, in order that more money might be left to my cursed elder brother, whom God confound! Jealousy, discord, fury, inhabit the monastery. It is true, I have preached a few bad sermons which bring me in a little money, half of which is stolen from me by the prior; the remainder I spend on girls; but when I go back to the monastery in the evening I feel ready to smash my head against the dormitory walls, and all my colleagues are in the same state."

Martin turned to Candide and said with his usual calm:

"Well, have I not won the whole wager?"

Candide gave two thousand piastres to Paquette and a thousand to Friar Giroflée.

"I warrant," said he, "that they will be happy with that."

"I don't believe it in the very least," said Martin. "Perhaps you will make them still more unhappy with those piastres."

"That may be," said Candide, "but I am consoled by one thing; I see that we often meet people we thought we should never meet again; it may very well be that as I met my red sheep and Paquette, I may also meet Cunegonde again."

"I hope," said Martin, "that she will one day make you happy; but I doubt it very much."

"You are very hard," said Candide.

"That's because I have lived," said Martin.

"But look at these gondoliers," said Candide, "they sing all day long."

"You do not see them at home, with their wives and their brats of children," said Martin. "The Doge has his troubles, the gondoliers have theirs. True, looking at it all round, a gondolier's lot is preferable to a Doge's; but I think the difference so slight that it is not worth examining."

"They talk," said Candide, "about Senator Poco-curante who lives in that handsome palace on the Brenta and who is hospitable to foreigners. He is supposed to be a man who has never known a grief."

"I should like to meet so rare a specimen," said Martin.

Candide immediately sent a request to Lord Poco-curante for permission to wait upon him next day.

CHAPTER XXV

Visit to the noble Venetian, Lord Pococurante

ANDIDE and Martin took a gondola and rowed to the noble Pococurante's palace. The gardens were extensive and ornamented with fine marble statues; the architecture of the palace was handsome. The master of this establishment, a very wealthy man of about sixty, received the two visitors very politely but with very little cordiality, which disconcerted Candide but did not displease Martin.

Two pretty and neatly dressed girls served them with very frothy chocolate. Candide could not refrain from praising their beauty, their grace and their skill.

"They are quite good creatures," said Senator Pococurante, "and I sometimes make them sleep in my bed, for I am very tired of the ladies of the town, with their coquetries, their jealousies, their quarrels, their humours, their meanness, their pride, their folly, and the sonnets one must write or have written for them; but, after all, I am getting very tired of these two girls."

After this collation, Candide was walking in a long gallery and was surprised by the beauty of the pictures. He asked what master had painted the two first.

"They are by Raphael," said the Senator. "Some years ago I bought them at a very high price out of mere vanity; I am told they are the finest in Italy, but they give me no pleasure; the colour has gone very dark, the faces are not sufficiently rounded and do not stand out enough; the draperies have not the least

105

resemblance to material; in short, whatever they may say, I do not consider them a true imitation of nature. I shall only like a picture when it makes me think it is nature itself; and there are none of that kind. I have a great many pictures, but I never look at them now."

While they waited for dinner, Pococurante gave them a concert. Candide thought the music delicious.

"This noise," said Pococurante, "is amusing for half

an hour; but if it lasts any longer, it wearies everybody although nobody dares to say so. Music nowadays is merely the art of executing difficulties, and in the end that which is only difficult ceases to please. Perhaps I should like the opera more, if they had not made it a monster which revolts me. Those who please may go to see bad tragedies set to music, where the scenes are only composed to bring in clumsily two or three ridiculous songs which show off an actress's voice; those who will or can, may swoon with pleasure when they see a eunuch humming the part of Cæsar and Cato as he awkwardly treads the boards; for my part, I long ago abandoned such trivialities, which nowadays are the glory of Italy and for which monarchs pay so dearly."

Candide demurred a little, but discreetly. Martin entirely agreed with the Senator.

They sat down to table and after an excellent dinner went into the library. Candide saw a magnificently bound Homer and complimented the Illustrissimo on his good taste.

"That is the book," said he, "which so much delighted the great Pangloss, the greatest philosopher of Germany."

"It does not delight me," said Pococurante coldly; "formerly I was made to believe that I took pleasure in reading it; but this continual repetition of battles which are all alike, these gods who are perpetually active and achieve nothing decisive, this Helen who is the cause of the war and yet scarcely an actor in the piece, this Troy which is always besieged and never taken—all bore me extremely. I have sometimes asked learned men if they were as bored as I am by reading it; all who were sincere confessed that the book fell from their hands, but that it must be in every library, as a monument of antiquity, and like those rusty coins which cannot be put into circulation."

"Your Excellency has a different opinion of Virgil?" said Candide.

"I admit," said Pococurante, "that the second, fourth and sixth books of his Æneid are excellent, but as for his pious Æneas and the strong Cloanthes and the faithful Achates and the little Ascanius and the imbecile king Latinus and the middle-class Amata and the insipid Lavinia, I think there could be nothing more frigid and disagreeable. I prefer Tasso and the fantastic tales of Ariosto."

"May I venture to ask you, sir," said Candide, "if you do not take great pleasure in reading Horace?"

"He has some maxims," said Pococurante, "which might be useful to a man of the world, and which, being compressed in energetic verses, are more easily impressed upon the memory; but I care very little for his Journey to Brundisium, and his description of a Bad Dinner, and the street brawlers' quarrel between— what is his name?—Rupilius, whose words, he says, were full of pus, and another person whose words were all vinegar. I was extremely disgusted with his gross verses against old women and witches; and I cannot see there is any merit in his telling his friend Mæcenas that, if he is placed by him among the lyric poets, he will strike the stars with his lofty brow. Fools admire everything in a celebrated author. I only read to please myself, and I only like what suits me."

Candide, who had been taught never to judge anything for himself, was greatly surprised by what he heard; and Martin thought Pococurante's way of thinking quite reasonable.

"Oh! There is a Cicero," said Candide. "I suppose you are never tired of reading that great man?"

"I never read him," replied the Venetian. "What do I care that he pleaded for Rabirius or Cluentius? I have enough cases to judge myself; I could better have endured his philosophical works; but when I saw that he doubted everything, I concluded I knew as much as he and did not need anybody else in order to be ignorant."

"Ah! There are eighty volumes of the Proceedings of an Academy of Sciences," exclaimed Martin, "there might be something good in them."

"There would be," said Pococurante, "if a single one of the authors of all that rubbish had invented even the art of making pins; but in all those books there is

nothing but vain systems and not a single useful thing."

"What a lot of plays I see there," said Candide. "Italian, Spanish, and French!"

"Yes," said the Senator, "there are three thousand and not three dozen good ones. As for those collections of sermons, which all together are not worth a page of Seneca, and all those large volumes of theology, you may well suppose that they are never opened by me or anybody else."

Martin noticed some shelves filled with English books.

"I should think," he said, "that a republican would enjoy most of those works written with so much freedom."

"Yes," replied Pococurante, "it is good to write as we think; it is the privilege of man. In all Italy, we only write what we do not think; those who inhabit the country of the Cæsars and the Antonines dare not have an idea without the permission of a Dominican monk. I should applaud the liberty which inspires Englishmen of genius if passion and party spirit did not corrupt everything estimable in that precious liberty."

Candide, in noticing a Milton, asked him if he did not consider that author to be a very great man.

"Who?" said Pococurante. "That barbarian who wrote a long commentary on the first chapter of Genesis in ten books of harsh verses? That gross imitator of the Greeks, who disfigures the Creation, and who, while Moses represents the Eternal Being as producing the world by speech, makes the Messiah take a large compass from the heavenly cupboard in order to trace out his work? Should I esteem the man who spoiled Tasso's hell and devil; who disguises Lucifer sometimes as a toad, sometimes as a pygmy; who makes him repeat the same things a hundred times; makes him argue about theology; and imitates seriously Ariosto's comical invention of fire-arms by making the devils fire a cannon in Heaven? Neither I nor anyone else in Italy could enjoy such wretched extravagances. The marriage of Sin and Death and the snakes which sin brings forth nauseate any man of delicate taste, and his long description of a hospital would only please a grave-digger. This obscure, bizarre and disgusting poem was despised at its birth; I treat it to-day as it was treated by its contemporaries in its own country. But then I say what I think, and care very little whether others think as I do."

Candide was distressed by these remarks; he respected Homer and rather liked Milton.

"Alas!" he whispered to Martin, "I am afraid this man would have a sovereign contempt for our German poets."

"There wouldn't be much harm in that," said Martin.

"Oh! What a superior man!" said Candide under his breath. "What a great genius this Pococurante is! Nothing can please him."

After they had thus reviewed all his books they went down into the garden. Candide praised all its beauties.

"I have never met anything more tasteless," said their owner. "We have nothing but gewgaws; but to-morrow I shall begin to plant one on a more noble plan."

When the two visitors had taken farewell of his Excellency, Candide said to Martin:

"Now you will admit that he is the happiest of men, for he is superior to everything he possesses."

"Do you not see," said Martin, "that he is disgusted with everything he possesses? Plato said long ago that the best stomachs are not those which refuse all food."

"But," said Candide, "is there not pleasure in criticising everything, in finding faults where other men think they see beauty?"

"That is to say," answered Martin, "that there is pleasure in not being pleased."

"Oh! Well," said Candide, "then there is no one happy except me—when I see Miss Cunegonde again."

"It is always good to hope," said Martin.

However, the days and weeks went by; Cacambo did not return and Candide was so much plunged in grief that he did not even notice that Paquette and Friar Giroflée had not once come to thank him.

CHAPTER XXVI

How Candide and Martin supped with six strangers and who they were

ONE evening when Candide and Martin were going to sit down to table with the strangers who lodged in the same hotel, a man with a face the colour of soot came up to him from behind and, taking him by the arm, said:

"Get ready to come with us, and do not fail."

He turned round and saw Cacambo. Only the sight of Cunegonde could have surprised and pleased him more. He was almost wild with joy. He embraced his dear friend.

"Cunegonde is here, of course? Where is she? Take me to her, let me die of joy with her."

"Cunegonde is not here," said Cacambo. "She is in Constantinople."

"Heavens! In Constantinople! But, were she in China, I would fly to her; let us start at once."

"We will start after supper," replied Cacambo. "I cannot tell you any more; I am a slave, and my master is waiting for me; I must go and serve him at table. Do not say anything; eat your supper, and be in readiness."

Candide, torn between joy and grief, charmed to see his faithful agent again, amazed to see him a slave, filled with the idea of seeing his mistress again, with turmoil in his heart, agitation in his mind, sat down to table with Martin (who met every strange occurrence with the same calmness), and with six strangers, who had come to spend the Carnival at Venice.

Cacambo, who acted as butler to one of the strangers, bent down to his master's ear towards the end of the meal and said:

"Sire, your Majesty can leave when you wish, the ship is ready."

After saying this, Cacambo withdrew. The guests looked at each other with surprise without saying a word, when another servant came up to his master and said:

"Sire, your Majesty's post-chaise is at Padua, and the boat is ready."

The master made a sign and the servant departed. Once more all the guests looked at each other, and the general surprise was increased twofold. A third servant went up to the third stranger and said:

"Sire, believe me, your Majesty cannot remain here any longer; I will prepare everything."

And he immediately disappeared.

Candide and Martin had no doubt that this was a Carnival masquerade. A fourth servant said to the fourth master:

"Your Majesty can leave when you wish."

And he went out like the others.

The fifth servant spoke similarly to the fifth master. But the sixth servant spoke differently to the sixth stranger who was next to Candide, and said:

"Faith, sire, they will not give your Majesty any more credit nor me either, and we may very likely be jailed to-night, both of us; I am going to look to my own affairs, good-bye."

When the servants had all gone, the six strangers, Candide and Martin remained in profound silence. At last it was broken by Candide.

"Gentlemen," said he, "this is a curious jest. How is it you are all kings? I confess that neither Martin nor I are kings."

113

Cacambo's master then gravely spoke and said in Italian:

"I am not jesting, my name is Achmet III. For several years I was Sultan; I dethroned my brother; my nephew dethroned me; they cut off the heads of my viziers; I am ending my days in the old seraglio; my nephew, Sultan Mahmoud, sometimes allows me to travel for my health, and I have come to spend the Carnival at Venice."

A young man who sat next to Achmet spoke after him and said:

"My name is Ivan; I was Emperor of all the Russias; I was dethroned in my cradle; my father and mother were imprisoned and I was brought up in prison; I sometimes have permission to travel, accompanied by those who guard me, and I have come to spend the Carnival at Venice."

The third said:

"I am Charles Edward, King of England; my father gave up his rights to the throne to me and I fought a war to assert them; the hearts of eight hundred of my adherents were torn out and dashed in their faces. I have been in prison; I am going to Rome to visit the King my father who, like me and my grandfather, is dethroned, and I have come to spend the Carnival at Venice."

The fourth then spoke and said:

"I am the King of Poland; the chance of war deprived me of my hereditary states; my father endured the same reverse of fortune; I am resigned to Providence like the Sultan Achmet, the Emperor Ivan and King Charles Edward, to whom God grant long life; and I have come to spend the Carnival at Venice."

The fifth said:

"I also am the King of Poland; I have lost my kingdom twice; but Providence has given me another state

114

in which I have been able to do more good than all the kings of the Sarmatians together have been ever able to do on the banks of the Vistula; I also am resigned to Providence and I have come to spend the Carnival at Venice."

It was now for the sixth monarch to speak.

"Gentlemen," said he, "I am not so eminent as you; but I have been a king like anyone else. I am Theodore; I was elected King of Corsica; I have been called Your Majesty and now I am barely called Sir. I have coined money and do not own a farthing; I have had two Secretaries of State and now have scarcely a valet; I have occupied a throne and for a long time lay on straw in a London prison. I am much afraid I shall be treated in the same way here, although I have come, like your Majesties, to spend the Carnival at Venice."

The five other kings listened to this speech with a noble compassion. Each of them gave King Theodore twenty sequins to buy clothes and shirts; Candide presented him with a diamond worth two thousand sequins.

"Who is this man," said the five kings, "who is able to give a hundred times as much as any of us, and who gives it?"

As they were leaving the table, there came to the same hotel four serene highnesses who had also lost their states in the chance of war, and who had come to spend the rest of the Carnival at Venice; but Candide did not even notice these new-comers, he could think of nothing but of going to Constantinople to find his dear Cunegonde.

CHAPTER XXVII

Candide's voyage to Constantinople

THE faithful Cacambo had already spoken to the Turkish captain who was to take Sultan Achmet back to Constantinople and had obtained permission for Candide and Martin to come on board. They both entered this ship after having prostrated themselves before his miserable Highness. On the way, Candide said to Martin:

"So we have just supped with six dethroned kings! And among those six kings there was one to whom I gave charity. Perhaps there are many other princes still more unfortunate. Now, I have only lost a hundred sheep and I am hastening to Cunegonde's arms. My dear Martin, once more, Pangloss was right, all is well."

"I hope so," said Martin.

"But," said Candide, "this is a very singular experience we have just had at Venice. Nobody has ever seen or heard of six dethroned kings supping together in a tavern."

" 'Tis no more extraordinary," said Martin, "than most of the things which have happened to us. It is very common for kings to be dethroned; and as to the honour we have had of supping with them, 'tis a trifle not deserving our attention."

Scarcely had Candide entered the ship when he threw his arms round the neck of his old valet and his friend Cacambo.

"Well!" said he, "what is Cunegonde doing? Is she still a marvel of beauty? Does she still love me? How

116

is she? Of course you have bought her a palace in Constantinople?"

"My dear master," replied Cacambo, "Cunegonde is washing dishes on the banks of Propontis for a prince who possesses very few dishes; she is a slave in the house of a former sovereign named Ragotsky, who receives in his refuge three crowns a day from the

Grand Turk; but what is even more sad is that she has lost her beauty and has become horribly ugly."

"Ah! beautiful or ugly," said Candide, "I am a man of honour and my duty is to love her always. But how can she be reduced to so abject a condition with the five or six millions you carried off?"

"Ah!" said Cacambo, "did I not have to give two millions to Senor Don Fernando d'Ibaraa y Figueora y Mascarenes y Lampourdos y Souza, Governor of Buenos Ayres, for permission to bring away Miss

117

Cunegonde? And did not a pirate bravely strip us of all the rest? And did not this pirate take us to Cape Matapan, to Milo, to Nicaria, to Samos, to Petra, to the Dardanelles, to Marmora, to Scutari? Cunegonde and the old woman are servants to the prince I mentioned, and I am slave to the dethroned Sultan."

"What a chain of terrible calamities!" said Candide. "But after all, I still have a few diamonds; I shall easily deliver Cunegonde. What a pity she has become so ugly."

Then, turning to Martin, he said:

"Who do you think is the most to be pitied, the Sultan Achmet, the Emperor Ivan, King Charles Edward, or me?"

"I do not know at all," said Martin. "I should have to be in your hearts to know."

"Ah!" said Candide, "if Pangloss were here he would know and would tell us."

"I do not know," said Martin, "what scales your Pangloss would use to weigh the misfortunes of men and to estimate their sufferings. All I presume is that there are millions of men on the earth a hundred times more to be pitied than King Charles Edward, the Emperor Ivan and the Sultan Achmet."

"That may very well be," said Candide.

In a few days they reached the Black Sea channel. Candide began by paying a high ransom for Cacambo and, without wasting time, he went on board a galley with his companions bound for the shores of Propontis, in order to find Cunegonde however ugly she might be.

Among the galley-slaves were two convicts who rowed very badly and from time to time the Levantine captain applied several strokes of a bull's pizzle to their naked shoulders. From a natural feeling of pity Candide watched them more attentively than the other galley-slaves and went up to them. Some features of their disfigured faces appeared to him to have some resemblance to Pangloss and the wretched Jesuit, the Baron, Miss Cunegonde's brother. This idea disturbed and saddened him. He looked at them still more carefully.

"Truly," said he to Cacambo, "if I had not seen Dr Pangloss hanged, and if I had not been so unfortunate as to kill the Baron, I should think they were rowing in this galley."

At the words Baron and Pangloss, the two convicts gave a loud cry, stopped on their seats and dropped their oars. The Levantine captain ran up to them and the lashes with the bull's pizzle were redoubled.

"Stop! Stop, sir!" cried Candide. "I will give you as much money as you want."

"What! Is it Candide?" said one of the convicts.

"What! Is it Candide?" said the other.

"Is it a dream?" said Candide. "Am I awake? Am I in this galley? Is that my Lord the Baron whom I killed? Is that Pangloss whom I saw hanged?"

"It is, it is," they replied.

"What! Is that the great philosopher?" said Martin.

"Ah! sir," said Candide to the Levantine captain, "how much money do you want for My Lord Thunder-ten-tronckh, one of the first Barons of the empire, and for Dr Pangloss, the most profound metaphysician of Germany?"

"Dog of a Christian," replied the Levantine captain, "since these two dogs of Christian convicts are Barons and metaphysicians, which no doubt is a high rank in their country, you shall pay me fifty thousand sequins."

"You shall have them, sir. Row back to Constantinople like lightning and you shall be paid at once. But, no, take me to Miss Cunegonde."

The captain, at Candide's first offer, had already

turned the bow towards the town, and rowed there more swiftly than a bird cleaves the air.

Candide embraced the Baron and Pangloss a hundred times.

"How was it I did not kill you, my dear Baron? And. my dear Pangloss, how do you happen to be alive after having been hanged? And why are you both in a Turkish galley?"

"Is it really true that my dear sister is in this country?" said the Baron.

"Yes," replied Cacambo.

"So once more I see my dear Candide!" cried Pangloss.

Candide introduced Martin and Cacambo.

They all embraced and all talked at the same time. The galley flew; already they were in the harbour. They sent for a Jew, and Candide sold him for fifty thousand sequins a diamond worth a hundred thousand, for which he swore by Abraham he could not give any more. The ransom of the Baron and Pangloss was immediately paid. Pangloss threw himself at the feet of his liberator and bathed them with tears; the other thanked him with a nod and promised to repay the money at the first opportunity.

"But is it possible that my sister is in Turkey?" said he.

"Nothing is so possible," replied Cacambo, "since she washes up the dishes of a prince of Transylvania."

They immediately sent for two Jews; Candide sold some more diamonds; and they all set out in another galley to rescue Cunegonde.

CHAPTER XXVIII

What happened to Candide, to Cunegonde, to Pangloss, to Martin, etc.

"PARDON once more," said Candide to the Baron, "pardon me, reverend father, for having thrust my sword through your body."

"Let us say no more about it," said the Baron. "I admit I was a little too sharp; but since you wish to know how it was you saw me in a galley, I must tell you that after my wound was healed by the brother apothecary of the college, I was attacked and carried off by a Spanish raiding party; I was imprisoned in Buenos Ayres at the time when my sister had just left. I asked to return to the Father-General in Rome. I was ordered to Constantinople to act as almoner to the Ambassador of France. A week after I had taken up my office I met towards evening a very handsome young page of the Sultan. It was very hot; the young man wished to bathe; I took the opportunity to bathe also. I did not know that it was a most serious crime for a Christian to be found naked with a young Mahometan. A cadi sentenced me to a hundred strokes on the soles of my feet and condemned me to the galley. I do not think a more horrible injustice has ever been committed. But I should very much like to know why my sister is in the kitchen of a Transylvanian sovereign living in exile among the Turks."

"But, my dear Pangloss," said Candide, "how does it happen that I see you once more?"

"It is true," said Pangloss, "that you saw me hanged; and in the natural course of events I should have been burned. But you remember, it poured with rain when they were going to roast me; the storm was so violent that they despaired of lighting the fire; I was hanged because they could do nothing better; a surgeon bought my body, carried me home and dissected me. He first made a crucial incision in me from the navel to the collar-bone. Nobody could have been worse hanged than I was. The executioner of the holy Inquisition, who was a sub-deacon, was marvellously skilful in burning people, but he was not accustomed to hang them; the rope was wet and did not slide easily, and it was knotted; in short, I still breathed. The crucial incision caused me to utter so loud a scream that the surgeon fell over backwards and, thinking he was dissecting the devil, fled away in terror and fell down the staircase in his flight. His wife ran in at the noise from another room; she saw me stretched out on the table with my crucial incision; she was still more frightened than her husband, fled, and fell on top of him. When they had recovered themselves a little, I heard the surgeon's wife say to the surgeon:

" 'My dear, what are you thinking of, to dissect a heretic? Don't you know the devil always possesses them? I will go and get a priest at once to exorcise him.'

"At this I shuddered and collected the little strength I had left to shout:

" 'Have pity on me!'

"At last the Portuguese barber grew bolder; he sewed up my skin; his wife even took care of me, and at the end of a fortnight I was able to walk again. The barber found me a situation and made me lackey to a Knight of Malta who was going to Venice; but, as my master had no money to pay me wages, I entered the service of a Venetian merchant and followed him to Constantinople.

"One day I took it into my head to enter a mosque; there was nobody there except an old Imam and a very pretty young devotee who was reciting her prayers; her breasts were entirely uncovered; between them she wore a bunch of tulips, roses, anemones, ranunculus, hyacinths and auriculas; she dropped her bunch of flowers; I picked it up and returned it to her with a most respectful alacrity. I was so long putting them back that the Imam grew angry and, seeing I was a Christian, called for help. I was taken to the cadi, who sentenced me to receive a hundred strokes on the soles of my feet and sent me to the galleys. I was chained on the same seat and in the same galley as My Lord the Baron. In this galley there were four young men from Marseilles, five Neapolitan priests and two monks from Corfu, who assured us that similar accidents occurred every day. His Lordship the Baron claimed that he had suffered a greater injustice than I; and I claimed that it was much more permissible to replace a bunch of flowers between a woman's breasts than to be naked with one of the Sultan's pages. We argued continually, and every day received twenty strokes of the bull's pizzle, when the chain of events of this universe led you to our galley and you ransomed us."

"Well! my dear Pangloss," said Candide, "when you were hanged, dissected, stunned with blows and made to row in the galleys, did you always think that everything was for the best in this world?"

"I am still of my first opinion," replied Pangloss, "for after all I am a philosopher; and it would be unbecoming for me to recant, since Leibnitz could not be in the wrong and pre-established harmony is the finest thing imaginable, like the plenum and subtle matter."

CHAPTER XXIX

How Candide found Cunegonde and the old woman again

WHILE Candide, the Baron, Pangloss, Martin and Cacambo were relating their adventures, reasoning upon contingent or non-contingent events of the universe, arguing about effects and causes, moral and physical evil, free-will and necessity, and the consolations to be found in the Turkish galleys, they came to the house of the Transylvanian prince on the shores of Propontis.

The first objects which met their sight were Cunegonde and the old woman hanging out towels to dry on the line.

At this sight the Baron grew pale. Candide, that tender lover, seeing his fair Cunegonde sunburned, blear-eyed, flat-breasted, with wrinkles round her eyes and red, chapped arms, recoiled three paces in horror, and then advanced from mere politeness.

She embraced Candide and her brother. They embraced the old woman; Candide bought them both.

In the neighbourhood was a little farm; the old woman suggested that Candide should buy it, until some better fate befell the group. Cunegonde did not know that she had become ugly, for nobody had told her so; she reminded Candide of his promises in so peremptory a tone that the good Candide dared not refuse her.

He therefore informed the Baron that he was about to marry his sister.

"Never," said the Baron, "will I endure such baseness on her part and such insolence on yours; nobody shall ever reproach me with this infamy; my sister's

124

children could never enter the chapters of Germany. No, my sister shall never marry anyone but a Baron of the Empire."

Cunegonde threw herself at his feet and bathed them in tears; but he was inflexible.

"Madman," said Candide, "I rescued you from the galleys, I paid your ransom and your sister's; she was washing dishes here, she is ugly, I am so kind as to make her my wife, and you pretend to oppose me! I should kill you again if I listened to my anger."

"You may kill me again," said the Baron, "but you shall never marry my sister while I am alive."

CHAPTER XXX

Conclusion

A T the bottom of his heart Candide had not the least wish to marry Cunegonde. But the Baron's extreme impertinence determined him to complete the marriage, and Cunegonde urged it so warmly that he could not retract. He consulted Pangloss, Martin and the faithful Cacambo. Pangloss wrote an excellent memorandum by which he proved that the Baron had no rights over his sister and that by all the laws of the empire she could make a left-handed marriage with Candide. Martin advised that the Baron should be thrown into the sea; Cacambo decided that he should be returned to the Levantine captain and sent back to the galleys, after which he would be returned by the first ship to the Father-General at Rome. This was thought to be very good advice; the old woman approved it; they said nothing to the sister: the plan was carried out with the aid of a little money and they had the pleasure of duping a Jesuit and punishing the pride of a German Baron.

It would be natural to suppose that when, after so many disasters, Candide was married to his mistress, and living with the philosopher Pangloss, the philosopher Martin, the prudent Cacambo and the old woman, having brought back so many diamonds from the country of the ancient Incas, he would lead the most pleasant life imaginable. But he was so cheated by the Jews that he had nothing left but his little farm; his wife, growing uglier every day, became shrewish and unendurable; the old woman was ailing and even more bad-tempered than Cunegonde. Cacambo, who worked in the garden and then went to Constantinople to sell vegetables, was overworked and cursed his fate. Pangloss was in despair because he did not shine in some German university.

As for Martin, he was firmly convinced that people are equally uncomfortable everywhere; he accepted things patiently. Candide, Martin and Pangloss sometimes argued about metaphysics and morals. From the windows of the farm they often watched the ships going by, filled with effendis, pashas, and cadis, who were being exiled to Lemnos, to Mitylene and Erzerum. They saw other cadis, other pashas and other effendis coming back to take the place of the exiles and to be exiled in their turn. They saw the neatly impaled heads which were taken to the Sublime Porte. These sights redoubled their discussions; and when they were not arguing, the boredom was so excessive that one day the old woman dared to say to them:

"I should like to know which is worse, to be raped a hundred times by negro pirates, to have a buttock cut off, to run the gauntlet among the Bulgarians, to be whipped and flogged in an *auto-da-fé*, to be dissected, to row in a galley, in short, to endure all the miseries through which we have passed, or to remain here doing nothing?"

" 'Tis a great question," said Candide.

These remarks led to new reflections, and Martin especially concluded that man was born to live in the convulsions of distress or in the lethargy of boredom. Candide did not agree, but he asserted nothing. Pangloss confessed that he had always suffered horribly; but, having once maintained that everything was for the best, he had continued to maintain it without believing it.

One thing confirmed Martin in his detestable principles, made Candide hesitate more than ever, and

127

embarrassed Pangloss. And it was this. One day there came to their farm Paquette and Friar Giroflée, who were in the most extreme misery; they had soon wasted their three thousand piastres, had left each other, made it up, quarrelled again, been put in prison, escaped, and finally Friar Giroflée had turned Turk. Paquette continued her occupation everywhere and now earned nothing by it.

"I foresaw," said Martin to Candide, "that your gifts would soon be wasted and would only make them the more miserable. You and Cacambo were once bloated with millions of piastres and you are no happier than Friar Giroflée and Paquette."

"Ah! Ha!" said Pangloss to Paquette, "so Heaven brings you back to us, my dear child? Do you know that you cost me the end of my nose, an eye and an ear! What a plight you are in! Ah! What a world this is!"

This new occurrence caused them to philosophise more than ever.

In the neighbourhood there lived a very famous Dervish, who was supposed to be the best philosopher in Turkey; they went to consult him; Pangloss was the spokesman and said:

"Master, we have come to beg you to tell us why so strange an animal as man was ever created."

"What has it to do with you?" said the Dervish. "Is it your business?"

"But, reverend father," said Candide, "there is a horrible amount of evil in the world."

"What does it matter," said the Dervish, "whether there is evil or good? When his highness sends a ship to Egypt, does he worry about the comfort or discomfort of the rats in the ship?"

"Then what should we do?" said Pangloss.

"Hold your tongue," said the Dervish.

"I flattered myself," said Pangloss, "that I should

discuss with you effects and causes, this best of all possible worlds, the origin of evil, the nature of the soul and pre-established harmony."

At these words the Dervish slammed the door in their faces.

During this conversation the news went round that at Constantinople two viziers and the mufti had been strangled and several of their friends impaled. This catastrophe made a prodigious noise everywhere for several hours. As Pangloss, Candide and Martin were returning to their little farm, they came upon an old man who was taking the air under a bower of orange-trees at his door. Pangloss, who was as curious as he was argumentative, asked him what was the name of the mufti who had just been strangled.

"I do not know," replied the old man. "I have never known the name of any mufti or of any vizier. I am entirely ignorant of the occurrence you mention; I presume that in general those who meddle with public affairs sometimes perish miserably and that they deserve it; but I never inquire what is going on in Constantinople; I content myself with sending there for sale the produce of the garden I cultivate."

Having spoken thus, he took the strangers into his house. His two daughters and his two sons presented them with several kinds of sherbet which they made themselves, caymac flavoured with candied citron peel, oranges, lemons, limes, pineapples, dates, pistachios and Mocha coffee which had not been mixed with the bad coffee of Batavia and the Isles. After which this good Mussulman's two daughters perfumed the beards of Candide, Pangloss and Martin.

"You must have a vast and magnificent estate?" said Candide to the Turk.

"I have only twenty acres," replied the Turk. "I cultivate them with my children; and work keeps at bay three great evils: boredom, vice and need."

As Candide returned to his farm he reflected deeply on the Turk's remarks. He said to Pangloss and Martin:

"That good old man seems to me to have chosen an existence preferable by far to that of the six kings with whom we had the honour to sup."

"Exalted rank," said Pangloss, "is very dangerous, according to the testimony of all philosophers; for Eglon, King of the Moabites, was murdered by Ehud; Absalom was hanged by the hair and pierced by three darts; King Nadab, son of Jeroboam, was killed by Baasha; King Elah by Zimri; Ahaziah by Jehu; Athaliah by Jehoiada; the Kings Jehoiakim, Jeconiah and Zedekiah were made slaves. You know in what manner died Crœsus, Astyages, Darius, Denys of Syracuse, Pyrrhus, Perseus, Hannibal, Jugurtha, Ariovistus, Cæsar, Pompey, Nero, Otho, Vitellius, Domitian, Richard II of England, Edward II, Henry VI, Richard III, Mary Stuart, Charles I, the three Henrys of France, the Emperor Henry IV. You know . . ."

"I also know," said Candide, "that we should cultivate our gardens."

"You are right," said Pangloss, "for, when man was placed in the Garden of Eden, he was placed there *ut operaretur eum*, to dress it and to keep it; which proves that man was not born for idleness."

"Let us work without arguing," said Martin; "'tis the only way to make life endurable."

The whole small fraternity entered into this praiseworthy plan, and each started to make use of his talents. The little farm yielded well. Cunegonde was indeed very ugly, but she became an excellent pastrycook; Paquette embroidered; the old woman took care of the linen. Even Friar Giroflée performed some service; he was a very good carpenter and even became a man of honour; and Pangloss sometimes said to Candide:

"All events are linked up in this best of all possible worlds; for, if you had not been expelled from the noble castle, by hard kicks in your backside for love of Miss Cunegonde, if you had not been clapped into the Inquisition, if you had not wandered about America on foot, if you had not stuck your sword in the Baron, if you had not lost all your sheep from the land of Eldorado, you would not be eating candied citrons and pistachios here."

" 'Tis well said," replied Candide, "but we must cultivate our gardens."